A Memory of the Infidels' Dance

J C Pereira

DEDICATION

To my wife and beautiful little daughter.

CONTENTS

ACKNOWLEDGMENTS

The core of this story lies captured from the fading remnants of a dream. Why my unconscious mind should draw on such a topic remains a mystery to this day. No doubt, current events influenced this creation and gave the body to the tale, which in its essence, is a romantic story. However, I chose to continue using past and current sources to expand on the setting. I desired to outline the triumph of love over unceasing adversity and not to make political comments. Unavoidably, these observations found their way into the book, but my primary intention was merely to give the romance a surrounding substance and a touch of reality. I hope readers enjoy the fictitious telling and remain unoffended by my inventions and reflections of outside events.

CHAPTER I

His long shift was over, and he was heading home. A numbness filled his mind, which fitted, hand in glove, with the monotonous drone of his clapped out, second hand, uninsured, ford sedan he was driving. It was all he could afford. Washing dishes and cleaning kitchen floors from one a.m. to ten a.m. did not result in a salary to live the elusive American Dream. He harboured no such illusions. He never did. He just wanted to get home, to that place where he tried to hide. That thought brought a slight twinge of hurt. His American wife, blond and brash, did not love him, but then neither did he, her. He was just a dirty immigrant, and she didn't know why she had ever let him touch her - lazy, good for nothing that he was. These were the harsh words he heard night after night. He knew that she was seeing someone else, but he did not care. His heart was beyond feelings. That was not entirely true. His little girl touched him somewhere deep down where he could not see, but it was remote. Her blue eyes, the eyes of her mother, would look at him, imploring him to join in with her games, to play with her as all daddies did with their daughters. He tried, but he couldn't. A cavern of regret and guilt separated them, tying him in place to a past from which he was still running. In the end, she would lose interest and walk away seeking entertainment in some other corner. He sensed the perpetuating harm he was cultivating by not fulfilling this little innocent's need for attachment. Somewhere on his downward slide through life, he had lost the vital connectivity to his self. He had no authenticity left – he was an empty vessel, incapable of saving himself, unable to succour his only daughter.

Cocooned within the oily smell and clattering noise of his car, he glanced absently over at the vehicle in the next lane, thinking to overtake the slow-poke in front of him. He noticed the four young Mexicans, all men, joking and laughing in shared comradeship. It brought back bittersweet memories from another place - a country where men were much closer together than a man was allowed to be in this machismo culture. He shouldn't complain, for it was in this land of opportunity he had sought refuge. Their joy in each other's company made him almost smile. He watched them as they sped off down the highway and clicked his indicator up to signal his intention to

1

change lanes. Swiftly, he cancelled his action as another car, a large dull black SUV, loomed out of nowhere. As it drew close, he recognized the occupants for what they were – hunters of men. He had seen them aplenty in his youth – men intent on killing other men, destroying dreams, shattering families through the barrel of a gun. He kept his place in the lane and tried to lose himself in the grating thrum of his car engine – merely another few miles from breaking down.

The surreal scene of ambush and murder unveiled itself to his unwilling eyes in a moment of clear vision. Only Allah knew what possessed him, for he gunned his protesting motor and slewed out on the SUV's trail. Horn blaring, he raced for the gap between the happy young men's vehicle and that of the one who intended them harm. In that suspended moment, he felt the surprised eyes of both sets of occupants fasten on his face. They had leached his features into their minds and had marked him for eternity. Without lingering for another second, he bolted off into the rushing traffic, breathing a sigh of relief. His inexplicable mad impulse lay in the tire stains imprinted on the hot asphalt behind him.

He thought nothing more of that hasty incident.

However, life is never kind to the oppressed, who are powerless to lift themselves out of the daily routine of existence.

The following day, he was once again driving home, chasing the repetitive cycle of deja-vu. People in this cruel world never forget a slight and go out of their path to seek vengeance without considering the consequences. Unfortunately, this attitude is the American way.

One glance into his rear mirror jolted his attention into his mouth, and he bit down on his pounding heart. That same black SUV reared up on his tailgate as a charging elephant bent on destruction, and his awareness was plunged into a kaleidoscopic, spiralling, slow motion of rending, squealing metal and shattering glass. His befuddled eyes focused down a gun's barrel as he sat trapped by the car's steering wheel, pinning him helplessly to the seat and his fate. He closed his eyes and waited for death – that long sought after release. Nothing happened, not even after that loud crack of sound.

'Are you okay, sir? Can you move?' shouted the patrol cop, his eyes wide open from the adrenalin rush.

Life still held on to him even as it let go of the man bleeding through bullet holes outside his wrecked car.

They rushed him to the nearest emergency centre, where a bored-looking nurse in a crisp uniform asked him if he had medical insurance. He shook his head, knowing what that meant in this land of privilege and inequality.

They quickly checked him over and declared him fit to go while his stretcher remained parked in the corridor, denied further entry.

It took him a long time to figure out where he was and, with his last few coins, bought himself a one-way bus trip ignoring the curious stares by the fellow ticket riders of his bandaged head and swollen face.

After an hour of enduring the many stops and starts, he got down from the city bus and took a shortcut that should take him to the street leading to his run-down apartment. He knew he had taken the correct route when he spotted the gay bar tucked away from the corner. It was an accustomed landmark to him, and he felt himself relaxing in familiar territory. In this world of mistakes, this was just one other. He saw the faces of the four young Mexicans staring at him in recognition, tequilas frozen halfway to startled lips. They had identified their rescuer and, in youthful enthusiasm, rushed over and surrounded him, inviting him to join in with their celebrations, whatever it was they were celebrating. He tried to refuse, shuffling this way and that to get around them, but they would have none of it, bullying him towards the bar's open front. They plied him forcefully with alcohol, and once he had tasted his usual solace, could not stop the flow of glass after glass, drowned as he was in the atmosphere of youthful laughter. His companions by entrapment were not innocent despite their appearances. They were toughs for hire, charged with dealing with any disturbances within the bar and had their fingers stuck in many a toffee pie. They stole the last of his freedom, and the alcohol robbed him of the remnants of his will.

The Spanish music played on in the background, a strumming guitar, teasing at something that lay coiled and buried.

'Come dance with me.'

It was an invitation that lacked meaning and came incongruously from a tattooed grinning face. A sly image, drunk with irresponsibility and bent on mischief.

The melody changed, the chords linking to a time that he did not want to remember. But one cannot deny fate. He found himself bound in the strains of forgotten music, and he lost consciousness.

The young tough, intent on persecuting his rescuer with his idea of irreverent fun as a show of his male dominance to his companions, lost control of his design. The foreign man, tall, thin to the point of delicacy, injured and intoxicated, danced, becoming one with the music of the rough youth's culture. He achieved this in a way that no native could ever attain, even those trained in it. His fluid, sensuous movements were on an ethereal plain – remote and untouchable. This surprise was sobering, but even more shocking to the young alpha male was that this man danced as a woman. He felt captured by the beauty of his movements. He felt the essence of his masculinity melting away and responded in the fashion of all males who sense a threat to their manhood – with anger. He stumbled away in confusion and belligerence and sat down among the confused and uncomfortable grins of his comrades.

The music played on, and the man danced on, both lost within each other, intertwined.

And so he found his place. He never returned home, just one block but an eternity away. His wife and daughter, abandoned and forgotten, felt better for it. They had gotten rid of the stranger who inhabited their space, allowing them to escape consequence-free.

This new dancer at the gay bar was not the same as the other dancers. He was at a level they could dream of but never achieve. He would select the patrons of the bar to dance with him as instructed, one by one. Those larger-than-life Americans, stuffed full of overconfidence who lived in ordinary families yet were unsure of their sexuality and place in the modern world. They covered their inadequacies with bluster and aggression, finding themselves drawn irresistibly to the alien interpretation of the most seductive and alluring steps of Spanish dancing. They could not wait but, at the same time, sat in dread of him selecting them to dance with him – anticipation and trepidation all mixed into one jar of potent alcohol.

The bar owner, a hard-eyed woman with a sharp glance for business openings, watched this tainted angel perform on her premises. His fame spread like a red stain through the community. More and more flocked through her doors. Bored with the mundanity of life, they desired to be captured and entranced by his otherworldly exhibition - women as much as men. She did not pay him, nor did he ask for payment. She just saw that he had food, had a place to sleep, and was supplied with as much alcohol as he needed to drown whatever sorrow he hid in his heart – ethical considerations did not exist. It was nothing to worry about, for the situation was but a temporary boon. However, ambition is an unpredictable beast.

One late night, he sat at the bar, quietly drinking as was his habit. She tended to leave him alone, but this night the curiosity building inside her inevitably spilt over and pushed her into intrusion.

'Who are you?'

He did not answer, no reaction whatsoever. The cynical proprietor was unsure as to whether or not he had heard her voice at all. She sensed that the only sound he ever heard was the music – haunting him from another place and another time. She latched on to that thread of opportunity. Tomorrow, I would like you to come with me. There is someone who I would like you to meet. Try and have a wash, though, would you?'

If she meant to be humorous or unkind, he did not notice. Once again, he showed no outward sign that he had understood her words or even heard her, for that matter. However, she did not doubt that he would come with her. He resisted nothing in this world and drifted along in whichever direction the wind blew. Only the music mattered.

CHAPTER II

Kabul is a place of uncertainty. It has always been so beyond living memory. Now, even worse. People wake in the mornings and go through the business of normality till night falls and bed calls. Everything has its rhythm, no matter how difficult the circumstances. Around every corner, surprises lie in wait. In this city, most are unpleasant, but some are also refreshing and ever-enduring.

Around such a corner, an accidental meeting transformed a young man's life.

He was rushing to the mosque when he collided with a young girl chasing after a toddler - a sure sign from the almighty Allah. It is forbidden to touch a female outside of your family in his culture, and they hastily jumped apart. He turned to bow to the older male walking behind her, offering profuse apologies for his unintended actions but not before he had caught a glimpse of her beautiful green eyes within the opening of her hijab. He expected a loud and vigorous public scolding and stood prepared to pay whatever compensation the transgression demanded.

The man walking behind, her father, was a man of unusual disposition and outlook. He sought to judge things not purely by the eyes but by the heart behind the action. In reality, he was well regarded within the community and was a good standing man — an upright man, an educated man, a doctor.

He regarded the flustered young man with sober, calm eyes devoid of righteous anger or outraged posturing.

'Young Abdul, isn't it? By my guess, you're off to morning prayers. I've seen you there on many occasions. I should be going there myself, but Allah has seen fit that I escort my impulsive daughter and uncontrollable son to my sister's for the day. On saying that, perhaps you owe her an apology for bowling her over, eh, young Abdul?'

'I, I...'

'Not to me, young Abdul. To her.'

'My sincere apologies for my rudeness,' he said awkwardly, not looking at the girl at all but keeping his eyes fixed on her father, which was correct and proper.

'Apologies accepted, young Abdul. To show that we forgive you, I would like to invite you to afternoon tea at my home. Do you know where it is? Do you accept?'

'I, I, yes. Yes, sir. I, I accept. Thank you.'

'Excellent! We will be expecting you after afternoon prayers. Don't be late.'

'No, no, sir. I won't.'

He took the chance to glance nervously at the waiting girl with the toddler now grasped firmly in hand and found himself swamped by her enchanting, dancing eyes.

The young man, Abdul, spent a nervous and distracted morning. He went through his prayers automatically without giving them the concentration and commitment that he should have and Allah demanded. Of course, this lapse didn't pass the notice of the Iman. However, the young man had lost his father to a tragic market bombing two years previously, and he tolerated the boy's sometimes absent behaviour. The unfortunate many-headed conflicts in the city caused not only physical injury but psychological and spiritual deformity.

Abdul appeared utterly unaware of the Imam's considerations and hurried out of the mosque after prayers with haste bordering on the blasphemous.

He found his mother and two aunts when Abdul returned to his modest home. It consisted of three rooms, a rudimentary kitchen, washroom, and a small, tiled inner yard. They were sitting in a circle on cushions laid out on a colourful Persian carpet, eating an assortment of nuts and discussing whatever it was they were discussing. He couldn't bring himself to disclose his invitation for fear that they would make far too much of it. He didn't know what to think of it himself and tried to remain calm.

He arrived at the doctor's home long before the appointed time and idled about outside, periodically checking his scratched and faded wristwatch, the last gift from his departed father. In his anxiety, he had foregone the afternoon prayers hoping that no one would miss him. The last thing he wanted was for someone to report him to the religious authorities as a worshiper in need of correction and re-education. Still, he was far too nervous to sit through the required prayer rituals. His mind lay much too preoccupied with what would happen after. If no one else did, Allah would surely notice that.

The dust lay thick in the air mixed with obnoxious pollution when he eventually knocked on Doctor Muhammad's painted, wooden door. The heat outside was suffocating and virtually unbearable. Much hotter than he remembered it as a small boy. Drought, among other things, threatened his homeland every summer now.

'Allah gives and takes away as he sees just,' he mumbled to himself to ease his tension.

'Ah, young Abdul. Punctual as London's Big Ben. Very admirable. Come on in. My wife has been looking forward to meeting you,' greeted the doctor, his warm, deep voice reassuring the highly strung young man as he ushered him through the open door.

Although unremarkable on the outside, the inside was large and spacious. They had decorated it in a tasteful Persian style, with a feeling of warmth and comfort emanating from it. The home represented the doctor – well-off, elegant but not opulent or pretentious.

His wife, sporting a simple, green headscarf, stood in a row with her children, waiting to meet him.

She surprised him by stepping forward with an open grin on her attractive face and shook his hand firmly, introducing herself before her husband could speak.

She then turned to her daughter and said.

'This is my daughter Jasmine. My husband tells me that the two of you have already met.'

His ears immediately began to burn with embarrassment, but when he glanced at the lightly veiled girl, he was shocked to find her appraising him quite directly and openly. He seemed to have lost the ability to speak, and thankfully, the good doctor rescued him.

'And, of course, that little rascal you're already familiar with.'

The two men sat on cushions around a low, dark wood, polished table and the women served them hot green tea then sat down to join them. It was all very unusually quaint and a bit foreign, but it made Abdul feel special. He hadn't experienced this feeling since his father passed away, and his family had to leave their high-status home to the modest one they now occupied.

'They tell me that you attended Kabul University,' said the doctor after they had their first sip of tea. He didn't elaborate on who they were but seemed unusually well informed.

'Yes, sir. I was studying economics, but my father died, and things changed.'

'Yes, tragic, but Allah is wise. We must trust in him. What are your plans now?'

'I have none. I am now my family's sole breadwinner, so I take whatever comes my way.'

'If you don't mind me asking, what happened to your father's stores, his business?'

'We had to sell them to pay off the debts.'

'Dear' piped in the doctor's wife. 'Why are you badgering poor Abdul about these sad affairs? I'm sure he would prefer to talk about something brighter, don't you think? Abdul, can you speak English?'

'I've always wanted to but never did get around to it for some reason or another.'

'Jasmine is a dab hand at it - learnt from her father's knee. Why not let her give you lessons?'

7

Once again, his ears betrayed him by turning bright red.

'That is very kind of you, Mrs Muhammad. I would be honoured.'

He did not dare look at his newly appointed English teacher, but he could feel her eyes on him.

'That's settled then,' declared Mrs Muhammad with great aplomb. 'Jasmine, my dear. Why don't you show our guest around our home? I'll prepare dinner in the meantime. You will stay to have a meal with us, won't you, Abdul?'

'I, I…'

'Of course, he will,' joined in the doctor. 'I have some business I would like to discuss with you, young man. We shouldn't make important decisions on an empty stomach, eh? Don't you agree, Abdul?'

'I…'

'Excellent, excellent!' exclaimed the doctor, clapping his hands together and rubbing his palms in satisfaction. 'I'll prepare my proposal while our Jasmine entertains you.'

Abdul's head was spinning. Something was happening, but what, he wasn't sure. Whatever it was, he was the main ingredient for his hosts were indeed cooking up something. However, it all had a pleasant feel to it.

Before he could think more in-depth on the matter, Jasmine rose elegantly to her feet and stood waiting for him.

Scrambling awkwardly to his feet, he followed her out of the room. A lamb led to slaughter. However, he was most certainly the willing victim, and he smiled inwardly as a comfortable warmth suffused him.

For the first time, he heard her voice. It rang strong and clear, yet at the same time, enchantingly female.

'You are not at all what I expected,' were her confusing words.

'I, I don't quite understand. What do you mean?' Abdul replied, trying to borrow time to figure things out. He had the feeling of a fly who had accidentally flown into the centre of a spider's web. It wasn't a sensation of danger, merely of being overwhelmed, out of his depth. This family was, at a minimum, unconventional, and at most, heretical. They also seemed to have a joint plan. What that was, he was almost afraid to find out.

'Your father and mine were friends and occasional business associates. Did you know that?' she said by way of an answer.

'No, I was entirely unaware. Did he talk much of me then? My father, I mean. I always thought that perhaps, I disappointed him.'

She didn't answer but said instead.

'When shall we begin your lessons? I was thinking every Wednesday afternoon after prayers. You can come here. Father is usually at home at that time.'

And so it all started.

After the short tour, he was guided back to a gently curried mutton meal accompanied with boiled rice mixed with saffron and raisins - all washed down with chilled water and augmented with flatbread and mixed salad. Between the polite yet informal chatter, he waited patiently for the doctor to make his supposed business proposal. Nothing materialized of this promise. As he surmised, they were all a bit odd.

In their presence, the harsh existence in Kabul with all its uncertainties stood suspended. It was a long time since he had felt so happy and contented with life.

For him, the evening ended much too quickly, and he returned to his modest home dominated by his mother and aunt. As soon as he entered the house, his spirit drained away, and a shadow of oppressiveness settled over his shoulders. The two women still sat where he had left them earlier that afternoon, and although they plied him with questions, he made his excuses and slipped away from further interrogation. He did not want them a party to his newfound happiness.

From that day on, he lived for Wednesdays, specifically for the hour after the afternoon prayers. He never missed his English lessons and was never late. His keenness lay not so much in the instructions themselves but the teacher. Her green eyes and her hypnotic voice held his concentration like the mongoose to the snake. As in all language lessons, the topics were many and varied, until one day it touched on Spanish culture and, of course, Spanish music and dance. These latter were forbidden topics and dangerous, but everything seemed normal and acceptable in the private bubble they had invited him to. What took place in that house never left its front door.

They were never left entirely alone. Mrs Muhammad was always somewhere close by - busily doing one chore or another. Her pleasant humming, echoing in the background - filling the spaces around them. The unidentifiable tunes, circling her daughter protectively. The doctor, although hardly ever visible, was felt through his presence. This laid back family ambience reassured him and made him relax in Jasmine's company, for the two of them together, unchaperoned, was improper.

Slowly, as time stretched on through many dinners, the doctor's business proposal leaked out between mouthfuls.

'Your father and I worked together, you know. Did I ever mention that?'

'No, but your daughter did,' thought Abdul, but he shook his head to the negative out of respect.

These words stood said in week two. It was becoming an established practice that Abdul shared meals with them after lessons.

'It's a pity you couldn't have picked up where he left off. I think this wish would have been his.'

Week three.

'Maybe you need a backer. Someone trustworthy to give you a head start.'

Week four.

'Perhaps things would be much easier if we were all one family, eh?'

That's when Abdul's food stuck in his throat, and his ears caught on fire. It took a lot of banging on his back and copious gulps of water to bring matters back under control.

'Are you alright, Abdul dear? How are your lessons going? Is he a good student, Jasmine?'

'He is usually a quick learner, but not always. The obvious sometimes escapes him,' she replied demurely.

Once again, his ears betrayed him by imitating a pepper. He was sure his teacher wasn't referring to his English abilities.

He now had a clear view of where this was going. Try as he did, he couldn't stop his heart from beating with the excitement of it.

'We have never met your mother, Abdul. We would love to have her over for dinner next Wednesday. With your permission, of course,' continued Mrs Muhammad.

Abdul didn't really like the sound of that. He felt as if the dream he was experiencing would touch the dour reality he was living and bring him rudely awake. He would prefer to keep his mother and aunt with their greedy pragmatism out of his newfound happiness, but the Muhammads had to follow specific procedures to meet acceptability. The laws of Allah demanded it.

From that point onwards, the river of events had only one course to follow, and Abdul was more than happy to sail his boat on it.

Before he could truly comprehend his change of luck, he had acquired a bride, become part of an honoured family, and had embarked on a business enterprise with a wealthy patron behind him.

The sun had risen for him in this country of war, instability and poverty. He intended to enjoy the warmth of its rays for as long as he could.

However, he had to remind himself that a man should not take his good luck for granted.

CHAPTER III

They arrived at a large parking lot, set aside from a busy dual carriageway. It had the feel of an island washed aside by a rushing river of asphalt, metal and plastic, transporting desperate and anxious humanity on a hurried path to nowhere.

A one-storied, sprawling concrete building sat in a far corner as if forgotten by modernity and the dreams of present-day America.

'Are you ready?'

Her passenger nodded, his face, as usual, devoid of any expression, his black eyes fixed on a distant place that no one else could see.

Inside, a guitar's rapid strumming and the staccato drumming of heels echoed from behind the partition of an inner hall. The gay bar's owner opened the double-winged door for her strange employee, and as they stepped through, the music with its intense, vibrant atmosphere swamped them.

The bar's patron could not stop herself from sneaking a glance at her companion. She needed to see what effect this consuming music would have on him. Disappointingly, his face remained impassive, but his dark eyes seemed to absorb everything inside the space, pulling its essence in. For the entire half-hour left for the advance dance class to finish, the tall, thin man with black hair hanging ungroomed to his bony shoulders framing a sad, angular, unshaven face did not move once from the position he had stopped in. He watched the dancers every turn and pivot, but at the same time, seemed ambivalent to their athletic activities.

After the students filed out noisily, giving the waiting pair perfunctory glances in passing, the dance mistress swayed elegantly over, her red clinging skirt moulding her firm limbs and hips evocatively and sensuously.

Her dark, beautiful eyes glowed with delighted recognition as she greeted her long lost friend.

'Elena, my darling, where have you been all these years?' she exclaimed with a strong, slightly husky voice.

'Chasing another dream, dear, but that's a long story for another time. You are looking as fit and ravishing as ever, mi querida,' responded the bar owner with a laugh.

For the first time since their arrival, the foreign man's inward gaze awoke in the present, pulled back by the two women's genuine warmth for each other.

'Then we have to find that time! Promise?'

'Promise.'

They hugged one another closely, eyes closed and submerged in the shared pleasure of united friendship, their warm bodies cementing the trials and loneliness of the missing years.

With a surge of will, Elena pushed the more graceful dance mistress away and said directly.

'I have a favour to ask, Caterina.'

A brief look of disappointment flickered across the face of the dance mistress, and she looked down her aquiline nose at the floor as if attempting to collect her equilibrium.

'For you anything, my darling. It has always been so. How could you forget?'

'I haven't. Life never turns out the way we hope it to. I'm sorry.'

'Hmmm,' was the non-committal response. 'What's this favour then, darling?'

'This is Afghan. We don't know the name he carries as he doesn't talk and refuses to communicate much. We shelter and feed him, and that is all he seems to want if that. Mostly, I think he just wants to die.'

Caterina focused on the tall, delicate man standing there immobile and vacant, her gaze searching but puzzled.

'I don't understand, Elena. Your introduction is a bit disturbing, but I can't see what it has to do with me. I'm not a social worker.'

'Bear with me, Caterina. He has an unusual and hidden talent. One you'll find fascinating, I'm sure. I would value your opinion on it very much.'

'Santa-Maria! You're taking my breath away. Common, stop with the suspense. Tell me what you want.'

'I want you to dance with him.'

'What!'

'Just dance. Anything. But it has to be Spanish.'

'That's a very vague statement, Elena. The music of the old country has many variants.'

'I know that. Trust me.'

Caterina looked deeply into her old friend's eyes for a drawn-out moment, then turned her gaze on the Afghan. As she regarded the still and seemingly uncaring man with a flinty professional inspection, her brow furrowed, and her eyes grew sceptical.

'Are you certain about this, Elena? He looks hardly able to stand.'

'Dance, Caterina. Dance.'

Shrugging her shoulders in resignation, Caterina turned quickly away, transforming once again into the brisk, strict, uncompromising dance mistress.

'Whatever,' she muttered under her breath.

Her friend smiled.

Without overthinking what she was doing, Caterina selected Francisco Tarrega, Capricho Arabe and touched the play.

The slow, intricate strains of the guitar followed her back to the waiting couple.

Taking a gentle hold of the Afghan's large elegant hand, she guided him to the centre of the hall. He followed her obediently and pliantly as a beaten dog led out of the kennels by his new master.

A second glance at the man's passive eyes filled her with doubt and drained her spirit, but a promise was a promise, and as always, she felt the urge to please Elena. She would do almost anything for her even after the passage of so many absent years. Above all, she was a professional, and finding that creative spark in her students was something she stood proud of and would never relinquish.

Erect and dignified, she started to follow the guitar chords trying to lead the lump of clay in front of her into taking a few experimental steps. He numbly shuffled after her, and she felt despair and some anger teasing at the back of her mind.

'This is just a waste of my time,' she thought.

Then like a snake uncoiling in the warm sunshine of a chilly early morning, he began to move, at first hesitant, but then, sinuously, his scales, glittering, reflecting in his awakening eyes.

Surreptitiously, he stole her control from her. Gently and intricately, he led her into the emotions hidden between the music's notes, capturing and liberating her simultaneously. She became his, lost to herself, and caught in an experience both erotic and exotic. The charged atmosphere, submerging her in the sadness of a country that she had only visited but from where her origins belonged – a culture, a people, family, love, loss, and regret. Entwining itself between all of this lay something foreign, exotic, orchestrated from the flowing, sinuous movements of a natural master – a phoenix reborn, a rising cobra, magnificent and untouchable in the sun's fiery rays.

Watching from the sidelines, Elena expected her friend to be surprised by the talent she held in her hands. However, what happened before her eyes was totally unexpected - even prepared, she froze, enraptured, overwhelmed.

From where she stood, she lay overcome. Tears flowed unnoticed and unchecked down her swollen cheeks as she saw the gradual possession of her friend by a being, risen out of the underworld. It coiled its ethereal essence around the dance mistress and turned her into a willing handmaiden, a servant of passion, a slave to his seduction.

She was once part of an elite dancing group in which Caterina had been the unchallenged leader, the best of the best. She had watched her awe audiences both small and large, captivating them with her expertise, interpretation and finesse, always pulling others into attempting to follow in her dance steps. She had never been privy to anyone ever succeeding, fellow dancers or imaginative audiences.

Now she was witnessing the downfall and, at the same time, the supreme elevation of this paragon of dance. She watched her dance as she had never danced before. All the elements that made that elusive perfect performance were there, but Caterina was no longer the architect of this achievement. The Afghan was wrapping her in the waves of his encompassing persona, denying her of her will. He seemed to be transforming her into his very own creation, or was it a re-creation? A rebuilding of something that was destroyed and only lived on in his damaged memories.

In all the performances that they had been in and seen Caterina in, she had never faltered. Even in practice, this had rarely happened. But now, in this exquisite and unusual partnership, she stumbled, a miss-step breaking the magic, and the music played on without them. The two dancers stared at each other on their island in the middle of the floor. He, once again blank and devoid of animation. And she as if hypnotized, her chest heaving with something other than exertion.

With an effort, Elena snapped out of the enchantment that held her rooted and, taking two unsteady paces forward, her thighs trembling with weakness, called out to her friend.

'Caterina?'

The dance mistress started as if suddenly woken from a vivid dream. With a nervous peal of laughter to cover her embarrassment, she hastily walked back over to the anxiously waiting Elena.

'Well?' asked Elena.

'Well what, darling?' replied the dance mistress, absently wiping the cold beads of sweat from her forehead with the back of one slightly shaking hand. 'He's quite a find, but I'm not sure I want to know any more.'

Elena glanced across at the still passively standing Afghan. He seemed unable to function without guidance from someone else. However, on the other hand, he appeared unconcerned by this predicament.

'Caterina, I want you to become a part of this! He is the key we could never find!'

'Is that why you ran away from us, darling? From me?'

'No, that wasn't it. I didn't mean that.'

'Whatever. Besides, I don't want any part of that man. Or, for that matter, any portion of whatever you're planning. I'm content with remaining a dance teacher. My dreams of past glories died when you left us. Let the past remain buried, yes?'

This last, she said with some bitterness, tearing a pause between them.
'You're not thinking straight at the moment. It has all been too sudden for
us - this man, his gift. It is almost too much for us to understand. Think
about it, Caterina. Dance with him once a week. That's all I ask - at my
place. I'll send you the address. You can continue to teach, and I won't
interrupt that.'

Her old friend's proposal rushed out more like a plea than a suggestion.
Elena had never pleaded for anything as far as Caterina could recall, for she
had always been practical, balanced, a born organizer. Passion was never a
part of her makeup. Of all people, she should know. This lack of
demonstrative emotion was the root cause of her frustrated efforts to win
her love. As they say, to try too hard has the same result as not trying at all.
The past was a carpet thick with sadness and regret.

'I'm not sure you know what you are asking, Elena darling. This man is
dangerous.'

'Dangerous? The Afghan? I've never seen him hurt anyone, dear. Except
maybe himself.'

'That's not what I meant. Listen, Elena, to dance with him is to lose your
soul. It's not magic but dark sorcery. I'm afraid, mi querida – terrified of
this power that he has. I don't want any man to have that over me.'

CHAPTER IV

It counted as one of the most beautiful days of his life. A memory he would always cherish in his heart until the last beat faded into death.

His bride was a queen, surpassed in beauty only by Soraya Tarzi, and he, a king. He felt the firm hand of Amanullah Khan guiding him between the beaming, joyous lines of the men and women of the households and their guests. Glittering and bejewelled were the women on the right and the left, the elegant and perfectly attired men.

The royal and stirring song of Ahesta Boro, the slow walk, caught his spirit and ascended his consciousness into the clouds. On that day, he had become more than an ordinary man.

They had already performed the Nikah before the mullah and were sworn man and wife as they stepped the path of the slow walk, joy enclosing them from every corner as they advanced to be greeted by a grinning doctor, his wife and Abdul's mother. Three times a vow voiced, intended to last for eternity.

The burning candles caught the embers in his soul at the high table and turned it into a flame of pure happiness. His beautiful Jasmine placed her small hand in his, and the night became a perfection.

They viewed their joint reflections under the shawl of togetherness and belonging and saw a future without the mar of ugliness.

Laughter and feasting surrounded them throughout the night, and at the end, they danced the Attan, swirling around the room in abandoned celebration under the gaze of Allah.

Heaven is sublimity, and marriage is just a rung below that. When a man joins with his bride for the first time, he becomes the happiest man in the entire world, a son of Allah.

That said, they were far too tired to consummate their joining and fell asleep side by side on their marriage bed, hands touching contentedly and fully clothed in wedding regalia. Of course, it didn't help that they were sleeping under Abdul's wife's parents' accommodating roof – a short-term situation he hoped. Not the best environment to unveil his bride's glories, much less enjoy them as a man should. Still, the image that lay behind his closed eyes before his dreams took him was the exquisite beauty of

Jasmine's delicate, naked face. Why should he long for paradise when he had already found it here on earth?

Weddings in Kabul are expensive affairs, but that sometimes financially debilitating generosity represented an invested stake in the future for all the stakeholders involved. The family was business, and such enterprises needed the family. One fitted hand in glove with the other, and his new relatives proved unstinting without fault.

A beaming doctor drove them through the chaos that was Kabul's traffic to a sprawling two-storey corner property. It sat there securely boarded up with its walls flaking and dust-coated, enveloped in an atmosphere of forgottenness and abandonment. The busy street that hustled by it no longer seemed to notice its presence, and it lay there forlorn in the bubble of a bygone time. Jasmine immediately fell in love with it, for she had the gift of seeing beyond the obvious. Abdul was more reticent, for although he had the imagination, he had untrained hands as far as physical work was concerned, and his means were minimal. However, above all, Abdul had a mountain of pride residing within his chest. The last thing he wanted was to be ever drawing on the well of his in-laws' goodwill.

'This ugly duckling, my children, is yours to transform into a swan,' announced the doctor happily, caught up as he was in the joy of giving.

He dropped the keys to the front door into Abdul's hands and left them to prove their worth.

'Call me when you need me,' he said in parting. 'But don't make it too soon, eh?'

The best gift is what you are willing to make of it, and Abdul and Jasmine worked hard at theirs both day and night. They set about scrubbing and cleaning the place from top to bottom. Then the scraping, sanding and painting. They started with the upstairs, for there would be the living quarters – a place to call home. At night, usually late, they would crawl onto the mattress in the corner, their limbs trembling with exhaustion and sleep the sleep of the dead. If it weren't for Mrs Muhammad popping in at odd times with food, they wouldn't have bothered eating a full meal.

One morning, when the heat lay like a suffocating blanket over a noisy, polluted Kabul, a knock brought Abdul reluctantly to the front door. At the same time, Jasmine positioned herself at an upstairs window to oversee the intrusion. A grizzled middle-aged man introduced himself as Malik, a master builder by trade, all muscle and gruffness. Abdul regarded him sceptically and asked him point-blank and almost certainly rudely what exactly he wanted, thinking him a roving vagabond in search of opportunity.

'Your father, the good doctor, has been good to my family and me, praise be to Allah. I am here to extend his kindness.'

'I'm not sure I understand,' responded Abdul, a puzzled frown creasing his forehead.

'The prophet said: The upper hand is better than the lower hand, I....'

'Malik! Is that you?' shouted Jasmine from her perch at the upstairs window.

Stepping back into the street, Malik squinted up at Jasmine, then after a studied pause, he replied.

'It certainly is, Miss Jasmine. My how your blossom has bloomed into the flower of womanhood. You are more beautiful than ever.'

'I'm wearing a chodri, Malik.'

'Yes, Miss Jasmine, but your radiance shines through it like the sun.'

Despite his forbidding appearance, Malik was a flatterer, and from then on, the door was always open for him.

He was also a skilful and dedicated worker, and under his guidance, their home and business premises lay transformed.

He invited them into his family with a magnanimous spirit, and his wife and their many children welcomed them with open arms.

No doubt, the good doctor was secretly rewarding the work he was doing for them, but that was not the whole story. Malik was a man fashioned by Allah without a stain of evil or ill will in his heart.

Within two months, Abdul and Jasmine's new home was ready and beautifully decorated. The downstairs space was a framework waiting like a chameleon. It lay poised to adapt to any front necessary for starting a new enterprise.

An invitation delivered by WhatsApp arrived, asking the young couple to a special celebratory lunch to mark the grand occasion. Jasmine had rarely seen her parents during this time, although her father's invisible guiding hand was always present. She was overjoyed, and Abdul was more than happy to return to more relaxed normality and discuss with his mentor and patron the following steps to take.

The appointed day arrived, and the doctor's house retained the warm feeling of home away from home to the newlyweds. Nothing seemed to have changed, and they ate lunch together in the usual happy and carefree way.

'So, did you enjoy laying down all that hard work to start your future?' asked the doctor.

'Yes, it's such a good feeling to be independent, or almost,' laughed Jasmine. 'But we couldn't have done it without Malik.'

Jasmine's casual, spontaneous remark then revealed the hidden business attitude behind the good doctor's geniality.

'Malik is a good man. However, in business, there are the givers and the receivers. This rule Allah bequeathed us. We should always remain careful not to cross that fine line, eh, Abdul? There is family. Then there are the others.'

'What do you mean, Daddy?' asked Jasmine, a concerned frown creasing her brow.

'Malik is an unusual and useful man, but he is indebted to me. We must not confuse this simple order. It may lead to unnecessary complications. Friendship has a price where business dealings are concerned.'

They all heard the warning but were uncomfortable in asking for clarification.

From that day on, they withdrew from the closeness they had cultivated with Malik's household. Malik, a man of gold, seemed to have understood and remained unchanged, but his wife, after her third invitation in a row lay avoided, became hurt by what she interpreted as rejection. This reaction remained unaddressed due to the discomfort of a potential confrontation, but maybe, in hindsight, it should not have been. But, the fall-out from that perceived slight still lay in the future.

The pause for reflection at the feasting table did not last long and the optimism of forming a new tomorrow consumed all present as if it were a drug.

'Have you given further thought to what products you'll be trading in, Abdul?' asked the doctor. 'It's time to fill all that space you have with something worthwhile.'

'We were thinking of a small food store specializing in the local markets. Malik, ah,' he stopped himself quickly. 'We've heard that the farmers outside Kabul are looking for merchants to work with.'

'You've just confirmed my point, young Abdul. Besides, everyone with a shop front is selling fruits and vegetables. That's a dead-end, I'm afraid. I have a better suggestion.'

And so it was. The good doctor, with his wise head, deep pockets and extensive if secretive connections, took control of the young couple's destiny and steered them into the uncertain world of money-making. They could not find it in their hearts to say no, for he stood well respected in the community for his generosity, and many people came to him to get help in dealing with the widespread obstacles to everyday life. He never charged a cent for this service, but it was impossible to stop the grateful citizenry from presenting him with gifts. He was always on his guard that others did not misconstrue these presents of gratitude, for he valued his good name and standing.

'Why not open a supply chain in building materials? I have modest contacts in this area. Many people here and in the countryside are trying to rebuild in difficult circumstances.'

'But even stone is under government jurisdiction. Isn't this the wrong area to invest in?' asked Abdul. 'My father once tried but was discouraged due to the difficulties.'

'Yes, you are right. The government did this to divert a potential free-for-all in illegal stone robbing. They need merchants with sensible heads to keep control of the situation. I happen to know a junior official who may allow us a tiny opening in this sector. I might add that such a responsible position will put you in direct contact with many householders and businesses requiring assistance. This opportunity would be a great help to me.'

Abdul was excited at the proposal, and he couldn't quite understand why Jasmine had remained so silent on the matter. When they returned to the privacy of their home, he broached the topic with her.

She looked directly at him, her eyes betraying a sadness he had never seen in their depths before.

'My father is not entirely what he appears, Abdul. I love him dearly, but you are my husband. He wants you as a stand-in between him and his many petitioners.'

'I don't understand. Is that a bad thing?'

'You are lovely, Abdul. But I think you are a bit of an innocent at times.'

No matter how hard he tried, she refused to say anymore, and he remained puzzled but not overly worried.

They threw themselves wholeheartedly into realizing the will of the good doctor and watched amazed as magical doors opened for them. In a month, their store lay stocked with building equipment which they spent most of their evenings studying their uses, and they had a minor government contract which entitled them to supply building stones and aggregate. It was an astounding success, and although bone-weary, Abdul was over the moon if oblivious to his accomplishments' improbability.

Within two years, Abdul found himself among the company of Kabul's businessmen elites and had gathered around him a small but continuously growing group of clients. As was the practice for unelicited favours, he received under the counter contributions for his efforts. In reality, most insiders knew that the real patron behind these good works was, in fact, the good, self-effacing doctor. The majority of the profits returned into his father-in-law's hands to pay off the investments he had made into their project. Everything was on the up and up.

'You do realize that we own none of this, I hope,' said Jasmine one evening when they sat preparing a late meal.

'Well, yes, of course,' he replied confidently. 'But we are all one family, aren't we?'

'Yes, Mr Musketeer,' she answered with a musical laugh. 'One for all and all for one.'

Despite the hard work and the ever-increasing demands on their time, their love for each other grew and grew. When the shop doors closed at seven-thirty sharp each evening, they jealously guarded their privacy.

They didn't watch television and didn't even own one. Sometimes the young couple continued with Abdul's English lessons, chuckling at his many grammatical errors and almost unintelligible pronunciations. However, mostly they listened to Spanish music and danced. Abdul was reluctant at first, thinking it sinful, but holding the joy that was his wife, inhaling her fragrance, was an irresistible allure.

The forbidden ambience of it sucked him in. He became lost within the arms of his Jasmine, her movements seducing his mind, his consciousness. And the music, the guitar, strummed its chords around his very essence. He became her, and she became him. Time became irrelevant and froze in their space. The only thing that mattered was the sensation of exquisite belonging.

They devoured everything that could add to this uniquely intimate experience, Spanish history, culture, dance, and music. So, when the couple danced, the knowledge acquired seeped in like osmosis into their shared and private performance, touch to touch, skin to skin, a slow electrical current.

There came a time when they couldn't wait to lay down the tools of their increasing success and retreat behind the curtain of their private domain. This moment defined their lives, not the accumulation of wealth that made their parents and sponsors so proud of them. It was foreign, and therefore, theirs only – a fantasy realm of their making, untouchable by life's probing fingers.

They were growing to resent their newfound high standing and the daily added names of nervously smiling petitioners. Everyone wanted something. Inevitably, the young couple and those who hovered over their shoulders had become the avenue for their gain. The relationship was deeply ingrained, a part of their society, but, at the same time, dangerously shallow—a bridge made of straws.

The couple thought themselves unnoticed. Secure in the bubble fashioned by happiness. What harm were the newlyweds causing anyway? What a man did with his wife behind the locked doors and four walls of their home was between them and Allah – no one else's business.

Life is not always kind. Whatever a man does, there is forever jealousy, misunderstanding, bigotry and resentment.

Even in the turmoil that is Kabul, one cannot imagine that the patch of existence that you inhabit can change on the whim of fate or a whispered word, for that matter.

The date was running up to 28th September 2019. Election Day was imminent, and an oppressive cloud of fear hung over the city. The diverse factions strived to influence their different agendas and objectives—some with promises, many with lies, and others creating terror. Power is money, and money is power. It was all there for the taking or losing, whether in the name of religion or good governance. The stakes were high, and the Americans watched it all with a hawkish eye claiming to be observers only, but one could not help but notice their well-armed troops on patrol. Handing out sweets to noisy children did not reduce the potential of lethal violence.

The good doctor's smile increasingly became strained as the results trickled in, and lunches at the in-laws soon degraded into monosyllabic affairs laced with tension.

Naïve Abdul may have been in many respects, but he was not stupid. He realized that his father-in-law's prospects lay firmly in the camp of the present status quo. A change would harm his fortune and, by extension, his and Jasmine's comfort. Already his clientele was beginning to dwindle. Those who still came were evasive and seemed to be playing for time, attempting to gamble both ways on the outcome. He was only a minor player, so he could not fully imagine the pressure the good doctor was experiencing.

When he tried discussing these things with Jasmine, she smiled enigmatically and said.

'We have to stay calm, husband, and perhaps keep a few bags packed.'

Many a truth stands said in jest.

The results of the election were not as bad for them as feared. However, there was still a lot to be desired from them.

Two of the participants claimed victory and the compromise consisted of sharing the ripe fruit of success – always a dubious solution in the long run. The interested third party responsible for claiming the allegiance of many young men, tired of being powerless and left without rights by those who said they were their defenders, carried on with the dark underbelly of terror.

One morning as Abdul opened his shop doors, he saw scrawled in red letters on his wall the damning writ of those who had nothing to lose.

'*Here stands the house of infidels who dances to the devil's tune.*'

The hot blood in his veins turned to ice water.

'Jasmine, Jasmine. Come quickly. Look at this!' he called out urgently, panic lacing his words with icicles.

His wife rushed out to him, and they stood there side by side, staring at the condemnation on their wall.

'How? Who could have done this? How?' whispered Abdul, the shock heavy in his voice.

'Come. Let's go inside,' replied Jasmine, her calm voice contrasting with the beads of sweat on her forehead despite the coolness of the early morning. She had forgotten to veil herself.

'Listen, Abdul. The tide has turned for my father - for us. Those who secretly resent him are emboldened, and the wolves are circling. This message is for our father, and they will drag us out into the dirt to shame him.'

'But they seem to know our secret. How? Who?'

'Focus, Abdul! It doesn't matter now. The cat is already out of the bag but, Malik is the only one who knew of our secret passion. That old man would never knowingly harm me, so he must have mentioned it to someone he trusts.'

'His wife! Allah protect us!'

'Allah only protects those who look to their own affairs, Abdul. We must go immediately to Father's. Shut the store.'

'But wouldn't it be worse there?' asked Abdul as he hurried to do his wife's bidding.

'Yes, but he will know how and where to hide us for the time being.'

The shrill sound of Jasmine's mobile scattered Abdul's already fragile nerves before he could complete the shutters' fastening that protected his property.

'Yes, um,' he heard his wife say to her mother. 'What! When?'

She listened keenly for about three minutes, her face gradually becoming as pale as a ghost.

'Okay. I'll be over as soon as I can,' Jasmine ended.

'Don't tell me more bad news?' asked a worried Abdul.

'My father has been arrested on charges of corruption. They will be coming for you next, Abdul. My mother says that you should give yourself up. That won't happen. My father is a sacrifice as a token of good faith to the Americans. Without a public stance against corruption, they will not support the President. My father will be in no position to help you, no matter what my mother thinks.'

Behind her logical assessment, Abdul could see that she was frightened and out of her depth. Still, he couldn't help himself from asking.

'What shall we do?'

'Run, Abdul. You must run. I cannot go with you. I'm pregnant.'

Abdul felt his whole body shaking, and his mind went blank as if it was overloaded and needed to escape.

'I have a cousin in Helmand province. He'll be able to help you. You must get to him as best as you can. I'll get you his address. He lives on the outskirts of Lashkar Gah.'

'Helmand? But…'

'Yes, Abdul. It's dangerous, and it's no place for a city woman. I love you, Abdul, but we haven't got a choice.'

He could see the deep sorrow and hopelessness in her green eyes.

'All you can take is a backpack with a change of clothes and money. We haven't got much time. They will be here soon.'

When she got back from preparing his pack, he was still standing there like a zombie, unable to move, unable to think, unable to function.

'Abdul, husband,' she implored. 'You are a clever man. You just don't know it yet. Survive! Survive for us. We will be fine. As womenfolk of the sacrifice, nothing evil will befall us. They will take all that we have, but they will not harm us. You will not be so lucky. If they put you in prison, I will never be able to find you again. Do you understand? Running is your only option. We will find each other again sometime in the future. Run Abdul and be clever, not just for you but for our child and me.'

Abdul numbly felt her warm, wet, salty kisses as she pushed him out the door. He didn't look back as he fled into the dusty, busy streets of Kabul.

CHAPTER V

'I won't dance for you!'

The words were emphatic and resounded with resentment and hurt.

'You're overreacting, Caterina. Think it through. It's not about us. We can't waste such a unique opportunity.'

'You're right, Elena dearest. If it were about us, I might have reconsidered. For you, it's about money. Simple. Gain has always been your motive, and emotion, friendship, and love meant nothing to you. I see you haven't changed. What a pity, eh? I'm sorry, but I won't dance for you, a puppet for your purse strings.'

'Look. All I'm asking is one evening per week. I won't take a cent from that night. I'll split the bar's takings evenly between you and the Afghan. Try it for a month. If you still don't like it, we can go our separate ways once again. What do you say?'

'Just like that, eh? And what about the Afghan, as you call him? Look at him, Elena. It's quite obvious that he doesn't even know where he is half the time. I won't be surprised if he can't even remember his name. He is a vulnerable adult, Elena, talented or not. Something inside him lies broken. God bless him. What you're doing counts as manipulation and exploitation. I think this whole sorry affair is unethical if not illegal.'

They both glanced apprehensively at the Afghan who sat on a leather sofa staring at nothing. No one could tell if he were listening to their heated conversation, and if he were, whether or not he even understood. He certainly didn't appear to care one way or the other.

'You may be right, Caterina. You always held the moral high road. But if you are, think about it. How is such a man to survive? The way he drinks, he will soon kill himself if some low-life doesn't kill him first. Can you imagine him alone on the streets of this godless city? I guarantee you he will be dead within a week. Do you want that on your conscience just for the sake of denying me?'

Caterina gave her old friend of yesteryear a long hard look.

'Convincing as ever, eh, mi querida? I'm glad to see you haven't lost your negotiating touch. How sad. Very well. I'll dance with this Afghan of yours, but not at your sinful place and not for your profit. We will return his skill to the people and God.'

'What are you proposing?'

Elena's tone was laden with caution. Perhaps too much so, for underneath, lay more than a hint of eagerness that crept up Caterina's spine, making her shudder. Rubbing her upper arms vigorously in an attempt to dispel the sudden rising of goosebumps, she replied in an almost disembodied voice. 'Since we cannot dance in the house of God, we shall dance in front of it. Why not at the bottom of the stairs outside St Mary's Cathedral, the old one, not the other. It's damaged and imperfect like all of us. There is little space, but we and our art belong to the old world, not this modern metropolis.'

Elena took a long time before replying, a worried frown wrinkling her high-domed forehead.

'Are you sure about this? It doesn't seem right somehow. A waste of time and effort.'

'Right or wrong, it is the only way you will get me to dance. What he has is only for God – an offering, a form of worship.'

'You weren't so religious in the old days, Caterina. If I remember correctly, you were scandalously sinful. I have no idea what has overcome you, but we'll do it your way,' said Elena laughing.

Caterina smiled back at her, genuine feelings for the collective memories. 'No, mi querida. I wasn't, but you have not danced with this man. He changes everything that you once held dear inside – he robs you of all that you have. He makes me afraid.'

'He's certainly made you melodramatic,' chuckled Elena, but this time nervously.

Passersby didn't know what to make of it at first. They wandered by with a fixed indifference to their surroundings, focused on preoccupations that had no relevance if they cared to look closer. Then against their will, something untoward arrested their attention. Reluctantly they paused, hesitant, their steps uncertain and faltering, unsure of whether it was appropriate to stop and stare or move on as if nothing lay there of any interest.

Never before had they seen such a display at the foot of their beloved Cathedral. Not a dicky bird or its cousin is free in this world, especially here in God's country. Their eyes roved around the couple, looking for the hidden catch. Maybe a mark to draw them in and empty their pockets of any loose coins within, a basket, a hat perhaps, to make a deposit: nowt, just an old disc player, spiralling music and two costumed dancers intertwining with exquisite elegance and coordination.

It was at that time of evening when traffic had dwindled off to a background trickle. Twilight laid down its hazy, indeterminate golden light and brushed stroked shadow over the great doors of the Cathedral, its edifice and the dividing pavement separating it from the street. On this narrow sidewalk, a stage lay set. A woman, proud of face, dominant, aggressive even, danced. Her arms stretched high, hands intertwining like animated snakes, her back straight and her firm seductive hips draped in a white, full ruffled skirt, crimson slashed, blouse, tied at the midriff, blood-red scarf. She moved sensuously as her long legs high stepped like a Spanish Andalusian horse – majestic. The haunting voice in the deep song of the Zambra by Estrella Morente surrounded her and lifted her movements through the cante jondo's beautiful highs and tight, low ends. The Flamenco guitars soared and swooped, accompanied by the mandolins, strumming out and plucking Middle Eastern melodies and rhythms – an ancient Moorish connection. The woman's swaying, energetic gyrations were hypnotic, drawing the onlookers like helpless victims into forming an encircling ring. She was an enchanting Gypsy girl plying her forbidden magic among those who dared to look. However, next to her, in the centre of her world, stood a consummate master. He stood dressed in tight black trousers, a white silk shirt covered by a black waistcoat with a brilliant red sash wrapping his waist, his long hair swept back into a ponytail. His slender form was immaculate and commanding – a matador at the height of his skills. He held the centre-ground, guiding and blending with his partner with athletic ease and expertise. His sinuous moves matched hers and coached their performance to untouchable levels like music spiralling out of the listeners understanding, taking the watchers minds to other places alien to them. They had never witnessed such an exquisite and unique interpretation of Spanish dance.

Those who were close enough tried to capture the look in the dancers' eyes – to catch a glimpse of their souls perhaps, to become a part of their excellence, even if only in a passive way. Her eyes were shining with an inner light, riveted on her enigmatic dance companion. He was the black hole to her burning star – a celestial partnership doomed from the start.

In contrast, his eyes were shockingly empty, devoid of expression, except for the tears that rolled from them down his high cheekbones. They could not know what memories were powering his artistic expressions. In his damaged mind lay a well of aching memories, unimaginable loneliness. In this inner universe lay an endlessly empty dusty plain, a mountain of majestic beauty sitting in its midst, and the image of a beautiful raven-haired green-eyed girl dancing over its craggy mist-shrouded summit.

They danced until the sun fell and the fluorescent luminance of the street lights illuminated them. The Cathedral's doors swung open to invite in the accustomed sinners to attend the evening mass, but the faithful no longer possessed the will to climb the stairway to salvation. They had surrendered to another type of deliverance – a tabooed spell of beauty, that of the fallen angels.

In the end, the priest and his acolytes descended into their midst. With loud voices and frustrated gesticulations, they urged the dancing duo to move on their way. The show had to end so that everyday life could continue without distraction.

'That was breathless, my lovely darlings!' panted Elena as she bundled Caterina and the Afghan into the back of her car. 'The two of you outdo yourselves each time you dance together. Incredible! I would pay a fortune to see you on stage.'

The two dancers seemed drained, and none of them responded, each lost in their respected thoughts – together, yes, but also alone.

That didn't seem to stop Elena or put her off in the least. The excitement from the evening's outcome and the resulting rush of adrenaline had her mind racing over the future possibilities.

'Where shall we go from here? What do you think, Caterina? You can't keep dancing on street corners. We have to plan this.'

Unfortunately, Caterina's following words threw a wet blanket over Elena's burning enthusiasm, frustrating her attempts on forming a promising enterprise.

'Take us home, Elena. We've had all we can take for today.'

'All right, dearies,' said Elena with a deflated sigh. 'We'll talk again tomorrow, okay?'

After a long pause, she continued.

'You both did well, Caterina. No matter what happens next, I will never forget this evening. Never have I seen its equal. You, he, are incredible! A once in a lifetime phenomenon.'

Despite her buoyed up mood, Elena experienced a twinge of concern and worry. As she glanced back to speak to her friend, she couldn't help but notice that Caterina held the Afghan's hand in hers, as if the dance teacher wanted to keep a physical link to him before she drifted away into nothingness.

'Not good,' she thought. 'Not good at all!'

Caterina was right. The Afghan was dangerous, for he carried cancer in the disguise of extraordinary talent. And this cancer was beginning to eat its way at all of them. The signs were already there. She and Caterina lay infected, each in a different manner. Yes, he could bring them that elusive fame and fortune, but he could also destroy them. She would have to be very careful with her plans, for all their sakes.

'We're here, Caterina. I'll call you tomorrow. We can talk then.'

The woman's eyes snapped open in surprise as if she had been dreaming somewhere else of something else - the dark kohl highlighting the largeness of her awakening and giving her face an eerie starkness, red-painted lips and white teeth.

'What?'

'You're home, Caterina. See you tomorrow.'

Caterina nodded numbly and, looking searchingly at the unmoving face of the Afghan, pulled on his hand, inviting him to go with her.

'No, Caterina. He stays with me. It is better that way. Tomorrow we will talk things through.'

Reluctantly she released the passive man's hand and, with a noticeable shudder, tore herself away and, a bit too hurriedly, exited the car, taking the scent of her perfume with her.

Without another word of goodbye, Elena drove away. She was not happy with what she had just seen, not one bit. But, on the other hand, she now had the leverage she needed. With every disappointment, there is an opportunity, as the old folk's so loved to say.

CHAPTER VI

'What do you see in me that you love so much, Abdul?'
'I love your green eyes, your warm beating heart, and your soul. You are all that I have been searching for even before I knew it. Allah is great.'
Her laughter pealed out, filled with joy, satisfaction and some degree of mischief.
'You are a romantic fool, husband. Someone has pulled you out of the stories from the old books. You do not belong in this place, this time.'
He looked back at her, his expression revealing his confusion.
She laughed again.
'Come, Abdul, dance with me. I know what music exactly we shall play.'

Without memories, we cannot exist, and Abdul would not have survived without that particular recollection.

He had lost track of how long he had been running. Every day seemed worse than the one before. Each time he tried to turn back, the casual cruelty of others barred his way.

Leaving the city had been easy enough. He knew the layout and had a fair idea of how things worked. His problems started at the first checkpoint he encountered.

In Kabul's reality, young men expect to be routinely shaken down by those who wear uniforms, the symbols of authority. Everyone is beholden to the one above, so exploitation begins at the street level. Police officers exercise their dominance over ordinary citizens, primarily young men, by taking what is not theirs under the guise of security. There was no shame attached to this, and it is merely business done in plain sight. The takings find their way upwards, hand to hand, through the chain of command and positions of importance. Everyone receives their cut. This corruption is the way of things.

Of course, as in all deeds, those disenfranchised, humiliated and robbed become fertile fodder. Such young men feed the ranks of those who desire to supplant suppression with yet another type of authoritarian rule. And so, the circle of war continues. One faction preying on the other, gain for some, exploitation, for others, an opportunity, for the rest.

Abdul knew these things. But when the usual stands shattered by the unexpected, common sense is suspended. No one in their right mind would ever contemplate traversing the unpredictable and predatory avenues of this troubled city with a bag full of currency. But, when his wife pushed him away from her embrace, he had stood bereft of a clear mind and sensible thought. He became a man cast adrift of his faculties.

Like everybody else, he used the mutat-i liani, the local transport, to get to the city centre. Although he felt as if all eyes were on him, no one gave him a second glance. Everyone had their troubles to attend. That was enough of a burden for them.

Huddled in his seat, not even noticing the suffocating diesel fumes, he watched the brightly coloured kites dipping and swooping as his bus drove past the occasional park. Bearded older men sat at the corners playing carrombul on faded boards and leisurely sipping green tea. Everything seemed so normal that he was beginning to think that perhaps he had made a mistake and he just needed to return home to Jasmine and open the store. Somehow he suspected that his world would never be the same again, and vulnerability settled around his thin shoulders.

He booked a place on the intercity coach at the bus depot, which turned out to be an aged, battered Mercedes-Benz vehicle without any air conditioning and windows half stuck closed or perhaps half-open.

Within an hour, he was on his way with much creaking and squealing of brakes. Despite the racket, he immediately fell asleep, clutching his rucksack against his belly for comfort, and woke with a start somewhere along a barren stretch of motorway. Fear struck him head-on when the coach, bouncing and shuddering, was pulled over and stopped at a security checkpoint. A fat, sweating official dressed in a stained police uniform climbed arrogantly aboard and walked along the aisle, wiggling his fingers at every passenger, not even bothering to offer the courtesy of looking at them. Occasionally, he demanded to know what individuals with bags were transporting and arrogantly proclaimed that the law required a fine for its onward passage. No one argued their rights, for they had none. Nobody protested the fairness of it, for such a thing did not exist. With a covert glance at the gun slung casually over the official's bulky shoulder, nondescript envelopes of varying sizes passed unquestioningly over into his grubby fingers, which he did not even bother to open.

Abdul did not fully realize his predicament until his turn came to be security checked. He found himself staring in incomprehension at the swollen digits wriggling in escalating agitation directly in front of his face. 'Papers,' snapped the obese guard, steadying the automatic rifle slung over his shoulder and placing his other hand on the holstered pistol at his waist. His intended threat was more than explicit.

'Let's see that backpack.'

Abdul sat frozen. He understood the mistake he had made, but now it was far too late to correct it. He should have predicted this, prepared for it. Unfortunately, his once privileged standing had left him unequipped for such an event. Knowledge is not always enough for survival. To his fellow passengers, such an eventuality was routine, a way of life.

'Hand it over!' shouted the guard, causing Abdul to jump in startlement.

A glance around told him that no one was able or willing to come to his aid. All eyes lay firmly focused on the floor of the bus.

Numbly, Abdul lifted the rucksack from his lap with trembling hands and handed it to the now glaring official.

Snatching the straps rudely from Abdul's weak grasp, the guard yanked open the buckles, ignoring his oiled weapon as it wobbled from his back to his ample stomach. Against his best efforts, his eyes widened in surprise, greed and maybe a bit of fear as he spied the contents.

'You have papers for this? Come, come! Get up! I am confiscating this. Come with me!'

It was clear that the guard was excited by his find, but he also stood unsure of whether or not he had stumbled across an insurgent. He was a bully, who enjoyed preying on the weak, and as all bullies go, he was a coward.

The barrel of his gun was now pointing at Abdul, his finger pressing nervously on the trigger – avarice and terror waging war within his jiggling chest. He needed to get Abdul off the bus fast and potentially talkative, now cowering witnesses on their way.

Suddenly, a man's head stuck through the opened bus door.

'Saran! Lieutenant! We've got company. Hurry!'

What was supposed to have been one ordinary day of business was turning into a mixed bag of dangerous snakes, one bit of nastiness after the other, for the profusely sweating policeman.

Not exactly knowing where his priorities for self-preservation lay, he rushed from the bus, forgetting the man he had been planning a summary execution to cover his theft and any repercussions, including the possibility of having rebels hunting him down.

'What's the bloody problem, now?' he snapped at his subordinate.

'The Americans, lumray Saran.'

'Allah protect us!' muttered the First lieutenant of police, then turning to the bus driver, he shouted. 'Get going! What are you waiting for a kiss!? Go!'

Following his fellow passengers' craning necks, Abdul could see a convoy of three reinforced and armour-plated Humvees bearing down on the check-point through the rear window.

Abdul never had a reasonable opinion of the Americans. Like all-conquering foreigners, they saw themselves as better than the Afghan people and did not seek to hide this attitude so convinced were they of their superiority. Yet, he experienced great relief at their fortuitous entrance.

Without their timely arrival, he would have been a dead man. Allah works in mysterious ways.

Still, his feet were far from out of the fire. In truth, they lay well nestled within the burning embers.

Without money, he wouldn't be able to buy anything, secure passage fares or, for that matter, pay the necessary bribes to get him to Jasmine's cousin. Lashkar Gah lay many miles away, nearly four hundred miles and walking that distance was out of the question – impossible even to contemplate. He would not have been in this dire situation if he had thought to take a flight to his intended destination. But, in hindsight, this sensible approach would now have him securely locked in custody. He was a wanted man, both criminally and politically implicated. The airport would have been the first place the authorities would check when they discovered that he was on the run. As Jasmine had said, they had made his father in law the scapegoat, an example to the international backers of their good intentions, a gesture of good faith. They would be thorough in this regard. Running along this route, uncertain as it is, was his best option. The checkpoint had been a close call, but the fat policeman had not been after him, merely interested in filling his pockets. His description would soon circulate, but the closer he drew to Helmand, the less likely the authorities would pick him up. Helmand was synonymous with hell for them, and the security forces on these lonely, exposed highways tend to be sparing and thin. However, because of this, other hazards, no doubt, lay in store for him. There were many disparate groups of bandits and militants along the way, awaiting an opportunity. Only Allah could protect him now.

Although he had a ticket to ride as far as Lashkar Gah, he would have to change, either in Jalalabad or Kandahar. The security forces would most certainly be checking bus passengers at both stops. For him to slip through their grasps would be an embarrassment, if only a minor one. Even if his assessment of his role stood overestimated, he could not afford to take the risk of negligence towards his safety.

It was beginning to dawn on him how little he knew of this land of his birth beyond the privileged circles he had travelled in. He professed to love his country and resented all outsiders decrying its culture, practices and standing, but what did he know of it and its people? Nothing. He felt ashamed and overwhelmed. The truth was that he had not cared. Not really. He said and talked about things but had not understood them. Now cut off and isolated from his usual comfort zone, he was beginning to learn.

Abdul had no choice but to sit tight until his bus pulled into its designated stop at Jalalabad despite these gnawing thoughts.

The scenery was harsh and breathtaking. The highway wound up through mountains and followed the winding path through river valleys, rock-strewn cliffsides almost devoid of vegetation on both sides, and in between racing white water rapids. Blaring from the bus driver's radio flowed a pulsing yet soothing Afghan tune, high and lilting, with lute, drum and melodic voices at foremost. Both the view and the music insinuated themselves between the worry in Abdul's mind and carried his troubles away. The occasional private cars, taxis and trucks passing outside his window added to the soporific atmosphere enshrouding him.

The multitude of yellow motorized rickshaws announced their entrance to the city of Jalalabad. There were twenty of the three-wheeled vehicles for every car, clogging the streets from end to end. In their midst, the bus, with all the other traffic surrounding it, crawled along. Pedestrians moved on all sides and in every direction, seemingly without aim like swarming ants on a bountiful nest. The noise, the smell of street food mixed with petrol and diesel, the bright colours of every tone, and the non-stop movement was unsettling disharmony to a stranger. Still, for an Afghan, no matter the ethnicity, it was as comfortable as home.

Feeling very much the hunted criminal, which he reminded himself repeatedly that he was not, Abdul descended the bus, trying to look in every direction at the same time.

He allowed the restless crowd to gather him up and sweep him away, instinctively knowing that he would be safest in the middle of the moving herd – colour and motion have always been confusing for a predator since the dawn of time.

Afghanistan has some of the poorest people in the world. Their plight and suffering have been overlooked by those who are lucky enough to have more than their fair share by the glib pronouncement, 'It's just one of those things, mate. What can you do? Nothing.' And so, the world looks away and carries on. However, in this pool of harried humanity where despair should be the word of rule, many gems roam around out there, refusing to lose their sparkle. Even with everything stripped away and hunger bites with every effort, the qualities that give humanity its place in the sun shines through. An old farmer, turban wrapped and front teeth missing, stopped his battered and poisonous rickshaw and offered Abdul a lift. Why he did this, not even the old fellow had an answer. Maybe he just wanted company and thought that this young, desperate-looking man would be adequate for the purpose. Perhaps, Abdul reminded him of a son he had never seen grown to manhood, lost as a child to polio or some other unconquered disease. The answer to that riddle would forever remain unsolved. The only point is that he stopped, and Abdul sent a prayer to Allah in thanks.

'Where're you off to, young fellow?' asked the farmer by way of introduction and courtesy rather than curiosity.

Honesty spilt from Abdul's tongue before he could stop it.

'I'm on my way to Lashkar Gah, but I've lost all my money.'

'Aiee!' exclaimed the farmer. 'This is something new for me. I've met someone worse off than myself. You see, I've never had money, so your pain is far greater than mine. Allah says we should be generous to those who have lost.'

Abdul wasn't sure if the ancient was making fun of him but decided to thank him anyway.

'I can't take you far, sonny, but I have a plot of land just outside the city. It's barely enough to grow some fruits and nuts. I just tried to flog some at the market - struck even but no more than that. If it weren't for my sheep, my wife and I would starve. They don't do so well these days. Thanks to our old Russian friends and their mines. Can't let them range as far as they used to, you see.'

The old farmer didn't seem to mind whether or not Abdul was listening. He enjoyed talking, and he had captured himself a one-person audience. He had a plan to keep him as well.

'My place is just two miles cross country from the Kandahar Highway. You're welcome to rest up there until the morning. We could use the company. I don't see many people these days. We're all old, you see. The youngsters have all gone to the cities. After a hard day's work, we old farmers are too tired for socializing. Not like we used to in the old days, anyhow.'

'Is that where your children have gone?' asked Abdul, thinking that politeness was the only decent thing he had to offer.

'Aye. I've had three sons. Lost two to land mines, and the other fled to Kabul. He runs a fruit shop, last I heard. He was always a timid, fearful soul.'

They were now bouncing and winding their way along a rough, dirt track pretending to be a road somewhere in the mountains. Abdul had no idea where and was utterly at the mercy of his garrulous host. It was also beginning to grow dark as the sun had fallen below the craggy peaks towering above them. All around him was dry and barren – dust, dirt and rocks. He wondered how the farmer's sheep found anything to eat, much less drink.

'The Hindu Kush, you see. Not so much snowfall as in the old days. No snow, no river, no water, no irrigation, you see. Allah's plan for us is changing with the seasons. He is testing our worth, I suppose.'

They soon emerged onto a flat, open plain and belted dangerously along a raised dirt road with neat rows of irrigated fields on either side. Trees whizzed by, planted to form an interspersed shaded avenue. In the dimming light, it all seemed green and fertile. For a city boy, it seemed like a fantasy version of paradise.

'Is your farm like this? Asked Abdul, already doubting the farmer's tale of enduring hardship.

'Nah,' replied the fellow, who was now concentrating hard on the road ahead. 'This belongs to the well-off villagers. They have fixed contracts with the townies, you see – easy life for them.'

They soon arrived at the hinted village, a ramshackle affair with houses made of roughly baked bricks and lights with naked bulbs glaring into the night. The few open-fronted shops were still open, and people, primarily children, were running around bare-footed on the rudimentary paved twisting streets.

Everyone recognized the farmer and shouted out good-natured greetings as he passed at a thankfully, much more sedate pace. Now surrounded by his people, the farmer took on a taciturn demeanour. Abdul got the impression that he was a consummate actor who enjoyed playing different roles for various audiences.

As soon as they got to the other side, which wasn't very long, the old fellow once again pressed his foot to the accelerator, and they tore along. Abdul gritted his teeth and hung on, trying to get reassurance from the observation that if the old farmer had survived to his grand age, then he must know what he was doing or at least lived a charmed life. Maybe some of that would rub off on him. Allah knows he needed it.

Outside of the headlights, everything was pitch black, but it wasn't long before the daredevil farmer slowed, careened around a corner, down a side path and skidded to a stop in a spacious open farmyard. Three grinning urchin faces immediately waylaid them, eyes peering curiously at Abdul. 'My grandchildren,' volunteered the old farmer before Abdul had the time to comment.

It was strange that the old fellow hadn't mentioned them before. Maybe his omission added to his concept of drama.

As if sensing Abdul's thoughts, the rascally farmer continued. 'Somebody's got to look after the sheep.'

Despite his seemingly harsh words, the three children, two boys and one girl, ran to him. He hugged them roughly and softly stroked the little girl's head. Under the dull yellow glow of the yard's light, it was evident that his affection for them was genuine and profound.

The home concept is elusive and has many manifestations, but Abdul felt the touch of homecoming caressing his heart. Who would have believed that out here in the centre of a diverse country that was his by birth only, he would experience such a connection – in the broom swept yard of a poor dirt farmer. Indeed, a person can only see with clarity when all pretences lie stripped away by unsought circumstances.

'I believe we're just in time for evening tea,' said the farmer, heaving his squealing granddaughter effortlessly up to sit around his neck and ushering his grandsons ahead of him.

'Come on, Abdul. These greedy little mouths will leave nothing for us, given half the chance.

Like his father in law, this insignificant farmer, in a village, like any other village, was the natural face of Afghanistan, opposites but in so many different ways, the same.

The farmer's wife proved to be a quiet woman, black-veiled and watchful. She welcomed Abdul to her fire because her husband had brought him over their threshold.

They all sat in a circle on the bare floor and, after a prayer of thanks to Allah, ate flatbread and vegetables washed down with hot green tea.

As hard as the stones that lie on his plot, the old farmer talked of succulent plants that he grew and nourished from an arid land with a bit of water. Meanwhile, his granddaughter laid her head on his knee and fell asleep.

With a practised smoothness that revealed a well-rehearsed household routine, the farmer's wife gathered up the children and disappeared with them behind a blanket curtain dividing a part of the room from the main. Her husband appeared not to notice and continued chatting to Abdul as was the right of men.

'You look tired, young Abdul,' he said finally. 'Sleep there. Tomorrow is another day, and if we are not here to see it, we will both be in Allah's bosom.'

With a laugh, he too disappeared behind the curtain, leaving Abdul at peace with himself for the first time since departing from his wife's embrace. He closed his eyes and dreamt of Jasmine's perfume. It filled his night and comforted him.

CHAPTER VII

Elena awoke troubled. She had dreamt of standing on a mountain of sand and feeling it collapsing under her feet. No matter how hard she tried, she just kept on sinking.

She had strong links with her community, where her value lay in her ability to organize. The community consisted mainly of Mexicans, Latinos and, like her, direct descendants of the home country, Spain. They all shared heritage and kept together to bolster themselves from the brutal reality of divisiveness that dominated daily life in the United States of America.

She had moved the Afghan into her home despite the gossiping whispers. She could see no other solution and didn't give two bits what other people thought. Her opinion on them was clear – no input, no say.

Caterina was becoming a woman unrecognizable. Her dancing was frightening in its passionate perfection. However, she fell further and further into a place that was destroying her after each performance. It was as if she were so intricately in step with the Afghan that he was dancing her into his inner hell. She was becoming more and more possessive. Separating them was a bitter battle each time they were together. She had graduated from pitiful and passive protest to tantrums and name-calling. Caterina was addicted to the Afghan just as he was addicted to alcohol and profound loneliness.

Elena could see the signs. It would all end in tragedy, which was almost a certainty. However, she wanted to salvage their coupling's unique beauty before they both fell into the abyss – capture it and display it for all the world to see.

She was canny and knew that she had to start small – wrap all concerned in light, gossamer strands and tighten them ever so slowly, pulling them together into the one spot where she needed them to be.

Caterina and the Afghan sat already committed. Hers to do with as she saw fit. They would dance anywhere and at any time once it was with each other – all to the tune Elena chose to play. She only needed to manage and dampen Caterina's escalating emotions.

The community was the next stage of her plans. She required them onboard to cement her dancing duo's growing fame – church steps had their uses but were far too parochial and limited. Besides, the high priests were unhappy with the enthusiastic crowds enraptured at the bottom of God's house with no inclination to rise any further. Fretful and annoyed, this heavenly body reported the foreign bacchanalia to the authorities. These upstanding and faceless gentlemen speedily issued a writ of regret and forbiddance. A licence was a requirement for busking, and anyway, this could not take place in front of the august cathedral. So that was that. She needed a new venue to advance her ambitions.

Her community was always grasping for things cultural, for it gave them a sense of worth that the hostile world around them was continually eroding. They had already bought her presentation. The only thing left was for her to work out how to profit from it without appearing so. It had to be a gift for the locals - sensationalism to make them strut and gossip with their fragile self-importance. That they were just a rung on her ladder must not be obvious. It wasn't that she didn't enjoy being with them. It was just that her discovery was far too great to be left merely for their entertainment and indulgent pride. However, they possessed the connections that she coveted. She couldn't prosecute her grand design without first going through them.

It scared her that she never knew what Caterina would pull out of the bag. So far, whatever her old friend and lover did, the Afghan always seemed one step ahead, as if nothing could surprise him or leave him wanting. The two of them didn't follow precisely a procedure of practice or worked out routines. They simply danced - each dance, a consummate performance. How could she tell the community organisers that she had something for them yet, at the same time, unable to say with clarity what that something was? There was no way for her to find out either. Whenever she probed Caterina, her response was a blank stare much worse than her previously fiery replies. She had no choice but to back off and hope that they delivered on the appointed day. Caterina had kept her word. They did not dance for Elena, and they never would. They danced for themselves and maybe for each other. Elena could never be sure.

She also had been unable to keep them physically apart. Caterina had made it clear that she would no longer go along with Elena's exploitative scheming unless she had access to the Afghan beyond dancing. She had had no choice but to leave the Afghan in her desirous hands some nights per week. Her previous partner's tastes always had a wider variety than Elena had a liking for. She guessed that Caterina was sleeping with him but how she managed to arouse that dead fish was beyond her imagination. He could dance like a demon, but otherwise, he was not a living thing. Something or someone had stolen or even killed his anima. God help them all, but she had to make this work, and she had no idea when this pot of gold would shatter into unrepairable sherds. Time was not on her side.

Still, in the meantime, smiles and occasional flattery done in a subservient ingratiating manner was part of her present armoury. She used these to disarm the overly made-up middle-aged dragons who controlled the Spanish community and, most importantly, the purse strings. Two of the most important had cornered her at one of the many fundraising events carried out in the name of the holy diocese.

'Elena, my darling, you must tell us what you intend. We have to know. Otherwise, we cannot present it to the committee.'

'Surely, you must have seen or at least heard of my prodigies causing a sensation on the stairs of St Mary?' replied Elena evenly.

'Oh, we have. Those two caused quite a stir. The bishop was very unhappy, even if everyone else seemed enchanted. I am not sure if we can risk offending the Church again.'

'Tsk-tsk, Olivia. Let's give Elena some slack. We also can't allow ourselves to miss such an opportunity for high cultural entertainment. We all know Caterina. She is an icon among us but this man, Elena. Who is he? He looks a bit foreign.'

'We call him the Afghan, but to say that he is a bit of a mystery, is an understatement.'

'Olivia's suspicions are correct then. He isn't Spanish – not one of us.'

'Does it matter, Ana? I have never met his equal in skill, Spanish or not Spanish. People flock to see him, more so than even Caterina, I think, but together they are unmatchable.'

'Yes, they are. Those two may be just what we need to get wider attention focused on our concerns. If their performance is a success, we may even be able to increase it into a roadshow or something far grander.'

'That's what I was thinking exactly,' replied Elena, but secretly her thoughts were not so kind and generous.

'If these powdered has-beens believe I will turn Caterina and the Afghan over into their clutching parochial hands, they have another thing coming,' she thought. 'One performance, maybe two, and then she would be moving on with the show. The high bidders would soon be approaching her. With luck, she would be able to sell the rights to the dynamic duo before it all exploded or, worse still, imploded. She had to work harder on Caterina to get her to sign papers making their working arrangements official. That wish was more strenuous than it sounded, for the unpredictable dance teacher could be a force of nature when cornered. She had found that out the hard way in the past.'

Caterina, despite her diligence and commitment to a work ethic, seemed incapable of handling fame. She craved recognition but was ever reluctant to take the next step. Elena had thought that she just needed someone to get her there and had taken it on herself to be her agent to success. But, just as they were on the threshold of that elusive outcome, Caterina had baulked at the idea. Completely at a loss to understand this lack of ambition, Elena had packed her bags and left. Well, fate had given her a second bite of that juicy apple, but now she did not harbour any romantic illusions. Elena would take what Elena wanted from the opportunity without hesitation. After that, she would go her solitary way as she had done before.

In the end, she got what she desired, a date penned in for a demonstration to the locals on the art of Spanish dancing. It was an indoor venue in the posh, gilded hall owned by the diocese, no less. When they had seen the opportunity to fill their coffers, they quickly became convinced of the project's goodness. Not so much as bringing in the flock but gathering up the wool. It was always surprising how thoroughly the glitter of coins could dazzle the keepers of God's house on earth, despite their heavenly claims and aspirations. Anyway, she didn't care two bits about what had swayed them. Things were progressing nicely. Tickets were selling like hotcakes, and the powder brigade was already bemoaning not having shelled out for a larger venue.

'Small minds should not be in charge of big projects, my darling bitches,' she wanted to tell them. 'You get what you pay for,' but she kept her mouth shut and smiled with the best of them.

As she had become accustomed to styling Caterina and the Afghan's talents, her progenies would be the centre of the demonstration, the star attraction. Supporting them would be the usual gamut of Mexicana-Americano brass bands and local two-bit dancers who had learnt a little from their grannies but didn't really understand what they were doing – the run of the mill noise and spectacle that would set the mood for her duo.

As usual, she was nervous, for she was a micro-manager, a control freak by nature, and Caterina was blithely keeping her in the dark.

'Stay out of our way, mi querida. You'll get what we give you.'

'The high stepping bitch!'

Elena did not have a choice, and she knew it. Staying out of Caterina's preparations, whatever they were, was her only alternative, and she could fume about it as much as she wanted.

The big evening had arrived with all its glitz and rows of special, well-turned-out guests clutching complimentary tickets, chief among them the once protesting bishop and his priests. But now, here they were in the balcony seats, accepting charity as if by right. Elena was furious at their hypocrisy but, as usual, hid it well behind gracious words and smiles.

Halfway through the show and she still did not know what the big attraction would reveal.

'It's a surprise, dear. Wait and see. I promise you won't be disappointed,' was Elena's standard reply to all the curious enquiries, disguising the fact that she wasn't any the wiser herself.

When the long-awaited moment arrived, she had to fight herself from feasting on her nails. So much pent-up anxiety resided in her that she felt imprisonment around her heart and ambition.

As a wild kaleidoscope of multi-layered, multi-coloured lace dressed local beauties sporting bright red lipstick and flowers in their dyed hair sashayed off to the blaring sounds of vibrant Mexican music, an expectant lull ensued over the vast chamber. Here, in this loaded pause, a group of musicians with classical Flamenco guitars and mandolins accompanied by women in Spanish dress filed in and began setting up their equipment. Then as the now-signature tune launched into the festive air, a hush fell over the audience.

'Olay!'

The plucky, flowing tune stringed jauntily into the silence punctuated by a rhythmic clapping, and the audience leant forward in their seats in anticipation.

In honour of Estrella Morella's famous Zambra song, Caterina and the Afghan had danced to this tune time after time on the steps of St Mary's and countless unknown street corners. It had become a part of them, and their adoring crowds had called for it over and over. It held them in the spell woven by the beautiful singer and the dancers' magic, one complementing the other.

'Que quieres de mi?'

The spiralling lyrics made them smile with remembered love, laugh with ecstasy, and weep with loss and sadness.

'Que quieres de mi?

Si hasta el agua que yo bebo te la tengo que pedir '

The dancers swept in, stepping and gliding through their routine, each time with a freshness of interpretation as if it were their very first seen performance.

The audience held their breaths, captivated. Only occasionally could a voice break through the enchantment with worshipping adulation.

'Olay!'

Then they were gone, leaving behind a burnt image on the retinas and a haunting echo in ears longing for an encore.

The entire hall rose to their feet like a storm surf breaking against the shore. A crescendo of noise – rapturous applause rising to the decorated ceiling as if in an attempt to call down God's attention.

'Olay! Olay!'

Without them, the stage lay empty even though other performers tried to fill the gap. Strive as they may, these gap fillers exactly knew what they were and tried their best with the realization that the restless audience was waiting only for what came after. Then the second act commenced, and the rustling of animated expectation stopped as if God himself had commanded silence.

They surprised them all.

In the dead quiet of the auditorium, sharp stiletto heels echoed, marking out a metronome of anticipation.

A statuesque figure emerged dressed all in black. Her top, a tight, body-hugging bodice, and below, rounded hips, draped in wave breaking layers of shimmering, ruffled lace. A long shapely leg, firm and enticingly muscled, half revealing, half concealing as she moved across the stage. An image, carved from ivory and exotically painted, the face of a courtesan bent on seduction.

She stopped, frozen to the spot like a marble statue from ancient Greece, poised, captured in stillness, caught in mid-motion.

Then the music. A song from a more dynamic land than the mother country. An inheritance from different cultures – a mix of continents. The expression of a people landed together in the pot of a foreign place across the ocean with hope in their hearts, fusing the things they loved the most, memories of joy, sadness, love, family and youthful energy – a taking back of what is theirs.

The music played, jarring, rhythmic, the staccato drum of Africa, the accordion, violin and piano of old Europe, a tempo of haunting vibrancy. 'Asi se baila - el Tango?' a voice of smoke, sex and rebellion – Veronica Verdier. 'So this is how to dance Tango?'

Then he appeared – erect, commanding, silk-white shirt, black sash and tight trousers, shoes to dance, an ensemble of outstanding simplicity, gliding onto the stage like a wraith of vengeance.

The crowd roared, and the battle commenced – as old as the bull ring, as ancient as the beat of the jungle, the sweat of passion; Spania! Italia!

As the frozen beauty spied her target, she broke her stasis and stalked towards him, shoulders pulled back and hips undulating sensuously. He turned to her, gaze locking, rising to his full height, a matador ready for the challenge. She stopped, raising her arms above her head sexily, hips lowered, leg curved and extended, stretched to tautness, showing him the entire length of her lithe but sensual body – a temptation irresistible. He reached for her, and she circled, her open palm on his ridged stomach, keeping him just out of reach, and the music twisted around them, drawing and releasing.

'Asi se baila – el tango?'

He reached for her, and she spun away, leaving her skirt ripped away in his grasp. He swirled it like a cloak, the fight capote, and flung it from him in a dramatic gesture of disdain. He needed no such defence – she was his to take. She pirouetted swiftly in succession, then halted, poised, beckoning to him with her eloquent fingers tipped by red painted nails – drops of blood in the air. Then they lunged at each other, passing, arms linked at the elbows, knees bent, legs extended – the accordion, rising and falling, in and out – a breath of sound, the piano, sharp, keeping tempo.

'Asi se baila – el tango?'

Straightening sinuously, linked for the first time, they danced, separate but as one, spinning and gliding. Not in the traditional manner of the tango. Not where the woman leant on and followed the man, unshakable trust, but as individual entities of passion and independence – a battle of possession.

They moved around the stage and through the strains of the music in effortless harmony, twisting, changing, legs kicking, flitting rapidly between each other, thigh draping thigh, intertwined and intimate – lovers fighting each other for dominance and control, proud and unbending.

Now unveiled of her lower wrap, her tight dancer's buttocks flashed nakedly from under her short skirt as she turned and spun in his arms. They danced for and with each other, eyes locked in intensity, and the audience felt both voyeurs and participants in this rampant exotic display.

The bishop and his priests looked decidedly uncomfortable in their front row seats but sat held fast, riding the compelling but unwelcome emotions and sensations rampaging through their threatened piety.

The dancers chased each other, first him, then her, catching, embracing, and pulling back – the game of love danced for all the world to see.

Then the finale. Elegant and powerful, Caterina leapt, held in her partner's arms, and with a high kick, dropped at his feet, eyes focused in adoration, painted lips parted in ecstasy.

There was nothing new here. It had all been done before in either one form or another. But the way it had been reknitted and executed was exhilarating and breathtaking in its uniqueness.

The audience paused to breathe, then broke into thunderous applause, especially the Argentinian contingent, memories of the old ports reawakened, shaking the entire room. Elena stood lost among them, carried away with the infectious enthusiasm.

'This is how you dance the tango.'

CHAPTER VIII

A week had gone by, unnoticed as the dry wind stirring the dust lazily in the farmer's yard.

Life is a bridge that takes you from one point to the next. It's not merely the crossing that matters, but how you choose to cross.

Abdul had almost forgotten the urgency that drove him. It lay hidden under the dirt that coated his unwashed skin and stained clothes, unsullied by the civilised city's politics and dishonesty. His fingernails, once so carefully manicured, now encrusted by dried mud - his odour, reminiscent of sheep and the hint of manure. He felt cleansed in a way that he had never experienced before, physically, spiritually.

He knew that he had to continue to Helmand, to Jasmine's cousin. Had she already alerted them to his arrival? His wife had assured him that she would be safe, and from what he knew of men protecting their power, there was no reason to believe that she would not. The sponsors would not take kindly to the dispossession and harassment of women. It went against the grain of public relations – the promotion of women primarily from the educated classes was a mirror to hold up to their public back home – smoke and mirrors.

He had decided on the first morning to stay with the farmer for a few days while sitting on the rough planking of the outside privy listening to the chickens clucking and pecking beyond the rickety wooden door that ensured a degree of flimsy privacy. Not that he had much choice. His pockets were empty, money, phone, gone the same way as his rucksack, and he had no ready means to grease his way to Kandahar or contact Jasmine. Helping the farmer would allow him a little space to think things through.

Well, he was still thinking. So preoccupied, he would get up early and walk two miles to the village. Once there, he would help out in the fields weeding vegetable patches belonging to well-off farmers whom his host continuously waxes disparagingly. Mostly, the women did this work, and he always took particular care to labour in a nearby field with the hot burning sun as his only companion. The money earned in this manner was not much. In truth, he had not been paid a cent as yet, but he intended to give the farmer half of his takings. In the end, Allah willing, he would be able to continue on his way.

At midday, he would walk back. Although the sun was at its most relentless, the shaded avenue of trees and the musical sound of running water in the irrigation ditches on either side of the raised, empty, dirt road made the journey a study in tranquillity. A peace would settle over his mind that made constructive thought impossible, and he began to fear these times falling under the suspicion that some unidentified countryside spirit was slowly robbing him of his will.

In the afternoon, he would help his garrulous host with his chores. In his trademark black turban, this harmless looking, grey-bearded man seemed more than keen to keep Abdul as a new member of his household. He wasn't as innocent as he appeared, Abdul slowly discovered. In his wayward youth, as he was fond of putting it, he had been a gun-smuggler in the Khyber Pass, working for either one or the other Warlord.

'We are all the same underneath,' young Abdul,' he said with a crooked grin that showed more gum than teeth. 'We fly different colours which are all interchangeable, but when it comes down to it, we are all outlaws, even those who call themselves the government. Allah sees everything.'

As the days slipped by into weeks and the weeks melded into months, Abdul began to think that the authorities had long since stopped actively looking for him if they ever were – he wasn't that important. However, sense prevailed and quashed the idea of returning to Kabul – might as well walk into an American enclave wearing a suicide vest than do that. It was time to move on.

Reluctantly he informed his easy-going host of his intentions.

'Abdul,' replied the old man. 'I've been all over this dramatic but unlucky country of ours searching for Allah's blessing. I finally found it here in this simple place. A man must do what he has to do. I hope one day to see you again before my eyes close for the last time.'

The morning that Abdul had chosen to leave, the old farmer took him in his evil-smelling rickshaw over back roads that, in reality, were only intended for goats and sheep and stopped after an hour's hair-raising drive at the side of the road to Kandahar.

With the appearance of a man who had all the time in the world at his disposal, the farmer remained at Abdul's elbow, waving at the intermittently passing trucks in an attempt to flag them down. He never seemed offended or discouraged when they raced by in a cloud of choking dust as if the two wayside would-be travellers did not exist. Neither did he seem to be affected by the oven that surrounded them, heat radiating off the rocks and asphalt with an intensity that withered Abdul's increasingly despondent spirit.

'Don't you worry, young Abdul,' he said in his usual affable way. 'The road to Kandahar will be here tomorrow, and the day after that, until our bodies have long become a part of this dust. As long as there is a road, there will be trucks. All we need is one to stop for us. Then our tongues can influence our fate.'

Abdul understood with clarity what he meant by that when a battered lorry with its cab painted bright blue and jauntily, some might say gaudily decorated, bounced to a stop next to them.

An unsmiling sun-browned face, turban wrapped, with fierce, piercing, blue eyes resembling the frigid waters of a glacier melt, glared down at them.

Unfazed as ever, the farmer stepped forward and weaved an incantation of sing-song words using Allah's name, striking a bargain with the truck's driver for Abdul's safe passage to Kandahar.

'Half now, the rest on arrival,' he finished.

Surprising even himself, Abdul stepped forward and swept the farmer into a hug that conveyed all the things he felt and wanted to say to the old rascal.

'Remember not to give him all the money at once, Abdul,' said the farmer hoarsely, tears in his eyes and at lost for words for the first time. 'Trust is a thing a person must gain.'

Clambering into the boiling cab, Abdul waved to his friend, sensing that they would never see each other again.

'Allah is truly great,' he thought. 'For even in a desert, a lucky man can still find an oasis.'

'We all have to leave our fathers one day,' said the driver with the devil's eye.

Abdul did not bother to correct him, for only the almighty knew if his mistaken observation had a mysterious truth to it.

The highway to Kandahar was a testament to how futile humanity's efforts were to leave an enduring mark on this world. What stood in recent memory as a proud feat of civil engineering was now reduced to a thin ribbon of mutilated asphalt. In the days' cauldron, the tar melted, and in the nights' sub-freezing temperatures, it hardened again. The signs of this torturous existence lay revealed by the deep, long ruts made from the wheels of the many passing vehicles, lorries, taxis and busses in their desperate dash across this no-mans-land of burning emptiness.

After ensuring that his first payment had lined his dirty palm, the blue-eyed devil fell back into his pit of silence, veined hands gripping the sticky wheel. The smell of the overheated asphalt, the diesel fumes from the truck's exhaust and the hot dust blown through the open window from the desert they were crawling through like a lost Dung Beetle filled Abdul's nostrils with a mixture that made him dizzy and slightly nauseous.

An old hand on this journey through hell, the driver, paid special care to keep his tyres in the grooves imprinted on the malleable tar. Although it seemed as if there was room aplenty on the sand dusted, road verges, he ignored the temptation and kept to the central route where trucks heading in separate directions, squeezed by each other with bare inches to spare. No one wanted to risk the bowels of their precious goods carriers, instruments of a precarious livelihood, disintegrating from the explosive force of an undetected or recently planted roadside bomb. Many a sand-filled crater bore testament to the demise of someone who did not pay this strip of despair the proper respect it demanded.

Blue eyes did not make a pleasant companion for the road. He was an individual beyond taciturn. The only time he showed interest in anything, but the length of asphalt in front of him, was when the helicopter gunship patrols passed overhead, rotors thudding ominously. These sentinel pass-overs occurred quite frequently compared to the Kabul to Jalalabad Highway. At these times, he would glare upwards, an icy, beetle-browed stare challenging the blazing blue sky above. He would mutter belligerently, but the only words carried distinctly to Abdul's ears were 'infidels' and 'dogs.' He wasn't sure if they went together.

Besides these airborne interruptions, the black road bored on for endless miles through a blasted expanse of sand, dirt and scorched rocks. Abdul felt as desolate as his surroundings. With nothing much else to do, he dozed off.

Something alerted him that things were not quite right. Most likely, it was the change in the surface which the truck was running over. The rhythmic drumming and humming of wheels over asphalt were no longer audible. He fought down the rising panic and the compulsion to leap upright in his seat to see what was happening. Instead, he pretended to be still in a deep sleep.

The truck came to a halt, brakes squealing in a complaint and the cab bouncing from over-sensitive shock absorbers. Harsh, commanding voices surrounded them, and Abdul risked a peek from one lidded eye. Dust swirled around in the space where he sat with the uncommunicative driver. The fellow sat leaning out of the open window fixing his gaze on whoever was out there. However, Abdul had slumped too low to make himself any the wiser.

'I've got another bird for your flock,' Abdul heard him say.

'Not like the other one, I hope,' someone replied in a harsh mountain accent. 'Got himself shot by a Yankee bullet before we could train him properly. This one had better be able to duck when told.'

Laughter followed this remark.

'Don't know about that,' came the deadpan reply from the truck driver. 'I thought he was the son of a dirt farmer, but the bugger seems to be one of those educated types.'

'Better put a bullet in his head now and be done with it then,' was the chilling reply. 'Save the Americans a bit of trouble.'

'That's up to you. I've done my part,' said the blue-eyed demon.

A loud banging on the door by Abdul's head put an abrupt ending to his pretence. He hardly had the time to sit up before a rough hand yanked the door open.

'Get out!' a voice commanded, and someone grabbed him by his shirt, pulling him rudely from the cab. He spilt unceremoniously out and barely managed to land on his feet. In his mind's confusion, he caught a glimpse of several men dressed in khaki and black, all turbaned and some with their faces wrapped. All were bearded and carried newly oiled Kalashnikovs draped casually on leather straps over their shoulders.

'A bit of a cat this one,' said another voice. 'At least the cockroach didn't fall flat on its face.'

'Make up your mind, Achmed,' ridiculed yet another voice. 'Is he a cat or a cockroach?'

'Shut your face before I do it for you!' replied Achmed nastily.

Abdul realized in whose company he had landed, and he was far from reassured.

The one called Achmed seemed to be the leader, but what this motley crew of dangerous-looking men wanted from him or, even more, intended to do with him remained an open question. However, he already had a suspicion lurking at the back of his mind.

'Get this truck out of here before it's spotted!' shouted Achmed at the driver. 'We'll settle up with you in the usual way later. Now is not the time.'

This conversation and vision were the last Abdul heard or saw, as someone behind him pulled a bag that smelt of old goat over his head and shoved him, stumbling in what direction he had no idea. His head swam from the stink and heat, and he had to struggle not only to stay upright but to suppress the vomit rising into his gasping throat.

He had no idea how long they forced him to walk in the stressed condition he was in. All that mattered was each laboured breath that felt half suffocation and partial drowning, all mixed into one foul bag that had become his entire world, his entire existence.

His educators had always told him that these people were a part of, yet separate from, Afghans like himself. They were children of the desperate, those fleeing the terror of the Russians, educated by the clerics on the other side of the Hindu Kush who embraces an extreme version of Islam. Now they had thrown off the yoke of their former controllers. Here they were, returned to the homeland with their uncompromising vision of the future. They were not to be trusted. They were to be feared, and Abdul was very frightened. They were not the disorganized, bickering and violent mujahideen of the past. No, they were something else altogether.

Finally, the blind, gruelling cross country dash came to a blissful stop, and Abdul collapsed, his leg muscles trembling with exhaustion. Grains of sand beyond count filled his shoes, and leaking blisters covered his feet. Had he a machete, he would have chopped off his limbs to get relief from the agony – or maybe not. Death felt a better option, for he had long lost caring.

'What is your name?'

'You know that already, Achmed. It's the cockroach.'

'Shut up,' replied the voice of Achmed tiredly.

Then the sun blazed into Abdul's eyes, blinding him. He cringed defensively, bringing his hands up.'

'What is your name?'

Taught courtesy from birth, Abdul tried to answer, but all that came from his throat, burnt livid and raw, was a pitiful croak.

'Give him a sip of water,' came Achmed's quiet command.

Abdul gulped at the warm liquid, thinking it was the most delicious nectar he had ever tasted, but the giving hand pulled it away before he could get his fill.

'Shall we try him with some sheep piss, Achmed?'

'Shut up. For the last time, boy. What is your name?'

'Abdul.' And the will to resist escaped with his name.

Abdul endured the implacable assessment by salt and pepper bearded Achmed. He had one eye, but that was enough it seemed for him to see all the doubts and insecurities that Abdul was trying to hide.

'Allah knows where that worthless truck driver found you, Abdul, but you're no farmer's son. You're soft and tender, accustomed to living under the shelter of the infidel invaders. What city are you from?'

'Kabul,' he answered without hesitancy.

'Thought as much. That den of iniquity, the underbelly of Satan himself. Your father was a merchant?'

'Yes.'

'University educated?'

'Yes, at Kabul University.'

'Well, you can forget whatever nonsense they've put in your head, Abdul. We will teach you what matters in this life, how to be a true son of Afghanistan. Learn well, and we will reward you. Practice deceit, and we will put a bullet in your skull. Is that clear?'

Abdul nodded numbly.

'Is that clear, Abdul?'

'Yes, clear,' he stammered, thinking that he had fallen into a nightmare and soon he would awake in the cab of that noisy truck.

No such luck.

'We will take you into the mountains and train you, Abdul. Then you can show us what you are worth.'

Abdul listened. Achmed sounded so reasonable. However, there was no mention that these bandits had kidnapped him into their cause – not even an opportunity to give consent.

'Are you married, Abdul?'

'Yes. My wife expects me to return in a day or two.'

'Are you a man or not, Abdul? Your wife will be there when Allah sees it fit for your return. If she is chaste, she will wait. If not, Allah will punish her, eh, Abdul? Come, get up. It's time to go.'

CHAPTER IX

Caterina was only too aware of her transformation, of what she had become. She likened it to falling into a dark place. There on those cold, hard rocks on which she crouched, she had found both liberation and damnation - the yoke of her Catholic upbringing forcing her to accept her fate as some divine punishment for undefined sins committed. Father, forgive me for I have sinned, continuously echoing at the back of her mind. At the same time, she exalted and revelled in her newfound artistic expression and the demonic catalyst that held her in its thrall.

She glanced over at the man at the centre of her ecstasy and torment. His body sat there like an empty shell awaiting possession. She couldn't stand the sight of him when he was like that, for it made her feel cheated and deluded. Yet, simultaneously, she trembled with fear when the music began to play. It signalled the end of her independence, her ability to be what she once was, a dance teacher in control of her fate.

At these times, her desire for him grew to an uncontrollable crescendo, in step with her talent. It burst out of her from corners she did not know existed. A volcano of white light pulsing to keep out the red. The more she danced with him, the greater her sexuality spiralled, and when the music stopped, the only way to find relief was to have him inside her. It was exclusively at these times that she could arouse him when the afterimage of whatever the music ignited still burned on in his head. The trick was to capture it before it faded, but it was never enough for her. She always wanted more.

It would destroy her in the end. She knew it but could not stop herself. She had jumped on the wheel, and it would spin her faster and faster until it threw her off. She had no idea when that would happen, but she intended to cling on until that final moment arrived.

Now, shamefully, the last thing she wanted was to be in his presence. He was a dead thing, and she had no desire for him in that state. All she craved was for Elena to come and collect him. It was always like this, the terrible lows after the soaring highs. In a few hours without him, she would be pacing the floors like a caged tiger, unable to continue another minute, desperately longing for his return, for the music to begin again, for the dance to continue.

'Come,' she said. 'Elena will be here in a few minutes. You must get ready.'

He did not move or acknowledge her in any way.

She forced herself to take his hand, forcing down the rising distaste in her throat, like acidic vomit, attempting to cleanse her of guilt.

His touch was cold and lifeless, alien.

'How could the same man evoke such fiercely opposite reactions in her?' she thought. 'It was unnatural.'

Even at the height of performance, the peak of passion - that exquisite point before climax - he never focused on her. His thoughts, his very being, swam in an ocean of memories where she would never belong. It filled her with jealousy, anger even, an inexplicable rage of rejection and resentment. In response, she watched herself, as if an observer, doubling her efforts to catch his attention, for him to whisper her name, a breath on her ear, but nothing worked. The more she tried, the further her sense of self slipped away, replaced by the poison of self-loathing.

The intrusive ring of her doorbell rescued her from prolonging the unwanted contact and destructive thoughts.

Dropping the Afghan's hand as if she had discovered she was holding a snake or worse, something dirty, she hurried to open the door, knowing that it was her condemner and liberator waiting on the other side. Only this root cause to her downfall held the key to free her, but she knew, had no intention of turning the lock to release her. Only through Caterina's emotional imprisonment could Elena realize her long-held ambition. Caterina had no illusions of what her ex-friend and lover indeed was – a hungry, ruthless entity lacking the genetic ammunition to achieve what she desired. Without manipulating those more talented, she would always remain in the shadows, unrecognized and unfulfilled.

'You're late,' Caterina hissed, her eyes sliding away from any contact.

'The traffic is a bitch at this hour,' Elena replied, trying a smile.

'Yes, it is,' came the sullen response.

'Is everything all right, Caterina?' asked Elena, genuine concern in her voice. 'Is he okay?'

'Afraid of losing the golden goose, mi querida? Don't worry. I haven't injured him. He is still yours to use.'

'That's not what I meant, Caterina. And you know it.'

'It doesn't matter. Does it? Go on. Take him. Get out of my sight.'

'I'll call you in a few days. Try to relax, Caterina. You look tired. Get some sleep.'

Caterina walked to the open door and held it, her eyes fixed on the floor, her face a semblance of implacable stone.

Sighing deeply, Elena took the Afghan's hand and led him away. He followed placidly, his eyes blank, his mind absent.

Caterina could not stop herself from glancing at him as his shadow passed, a fleet look of hope in her quick gaze. He did not notice.

In disgust, she slammed the door behind them with what she hoped was a defiant gesture of finality.

Feeling wholly worthless and unclean, she robotically poured herself a hot bath, her thoughts sliding away from her like wet mud from a wall. She had isolated herself, refusing to answer the growing urgent calls from her mother and sister. Thank small mercies, they lived in another city on the other side of the country. She couldn't cope with them bursting in on her unannounced with panic chasing them like squawking chickens.

Soon enveloped by the steaming water, she felt the tension holding her body together beginning to ease and wondered if she would melt into the liquid surrounding her. That made her laugh, and she felt better.

Sleep came quickly after that, and when she woke, vibrant energy drove her from her bed, her mind feverishly planning the next performance with the Afghan.

'God, I wish I knew his name! Is it possible to be so close to a man and not knowing what his mother called him?'

Maybe names are for what you are inside and belonged to more than just the physical level. Since Caterina knew nothing about the Afghan entirely, that vague reference would have to do.

Anyway, she had more important things about which to think. The next performance was going to be the biggest one yet, according to that conniving bitch Elena. She hadn't divulged any of the details to Caterina. Tit for tat, she assumed, as her spiteful ex-lover did not like how Caterina kept her in the dark about the choice of choreographing and what she felt and did with the Afghan in private. 'So childish!' she thought, her mind buzzing with electrical activity.

She resisted the compelling urge to ring Elena with the pretence to bring the Afghan over for practice, but she would see through her ruse. They hardly did that, for he would mostly stand there staring stupidly at her, arms dangling at his side. Now and again, if by random she managed to hit on a precise musical selection, he would come alive. At these times, he never forgot the sequence and never made a mistake or false step during the actual performance. She knew he was not dancing with her. By now, she had come to realize that he was dancing with someone else - holding someone who meant all the world to him, more than life itself. He was not thinking or reliving the past. He was in the past. She, to all intent and purpose, did not exist. The thread that held his sanity tethered to the now had snapped, and he had fled to another world. A secure place that was his before whatever unknown trauma shattered him.

'Poor Afghan,' she thought.

Incongruously, in that very moment, an uncontrollable desire overcame her, filling her loins with a flood of heat and stripping away her breath. All she wanted was to feel him under her hands, his firm, muscled body moving with hers, the music shuddering and beating in time with their steps.

She was an addict. As helpless in directing her fate as the lost soul in the shadow of a damp underpass. Curled up and forsaken, hanging on in the hope of subsequent euphoria in the form of a sharp prick in a vein. Her needle was the Afghan, and she needed him desperately. Her drug was to dance with him.

She tried to stay occupied, returning to her classes as if they still mattered. Her students, she noticed, now viewed her in a different light. As if she were an archangel, perhaps Lucifer, or maybe a Watcher's daughter from the book of Enoch, manifested among their company like a heavenly vision. She felt that if she were to instruct them to dance out of an open window on the sixth floor, they would do it happily. Maybe she should try it for a laugh.

On her part, things had also changed. She saw her once sparkling prodigies as dull automatons with feet of clay – earth plodders with unattainable aspirations to fly. It took all of her self-control and a lot of lip biting to stop herself from shouting at them in frustration. At times, she just wanted them to get out, to disappear from her sight. Their pitiful need to catch her attention and receive nods of approval for mediocre attainments made her sick to her stomach.

Her life's work, the thing that had given her solace and meaning in her wilderness years, was crumbling under her lace tied shoes. She wanted to let implacable gravity have its way but was afraid of the hole it would create – of falling into the void of nothingness.

She managed to hold out for a week, then unable to stand the ants running over her brain and under her skin any longer, she touched the mocking image of Elena displayed on her phone.

'That took you long enough, dear. Have you got what we need?'

Caterina tried to swallow the heated anger, which was increasingly escalating into hate, down her burning throat and into her stomach. Almost. Her reply was biting and laced with vinegar.

'By that, you mean do I have a choreographed piece that you can exploit as you lack the skill to do it yourself?'

Laughter crackled down the mobile, but there was enough spiteful hurt in it to give some satisfaction.

'Pull those claws in, mi querida. But, yes, something like that. Well?'

'Well, what?'

'Don't be coy, dear. A simple yes or no will do.'

'I have a loose idea, but I need the star of the show to see if it will work. Bring him over.'

'Of course, darling. But try and use your energy on the work if you can.'

More laughter followed.

'We'll be over bright and early tomorrow morning. I'll need the time to sober up twinkle toes. The darling can hardly stand at the moment.'

'Have you got a new venue for us?'

'You do your part, mi querida, and I'll deliver mine. See you tomorrow.'

And the connection went dead.

Caterina grimaced and stood there at the stretching bar tapping a rhythm of frustration on the hardwood with her fingers.

'She had to do something, and soon,' she thought, but what, she had no idea.

The unexpected call had come two days ago - the voice on the phone full of duplicity and falseness, smiles and kind words hiding a darker side, self-interest and greed wrapped in cleverness. A part of Caterina's past she had long thought safely buried – graverobbers never fail to spot an opportunity. 'We have been following you,' the voice said. 'Documenting your progress – your splendid rise. We have not seen anything like your performances in a long time – too long. We would love to make you an offer – a contract of mutual benefit that we would make worth your while.'

As in the old days, her speech had dried up, her thoughts emptied, her wit blown away in a sudden wind of surprise.

'I, I don't know,' she had answered. 'I don't usually handle these things. You will have to speak to my agent and manager.'

'Ah, of course. I understand. Are you able to give us a name and number?'

'I prefer to speak to her first if you don't mind. Leave me your name, number and who you represent,' she said, always good at buying time. 'We will call you to hear what you have to say after we've discussed matters.'

'Excellent! We are excited at the prospect of working with you. If you give me your email, I will send you our details.'

Elena was of their ilk. This world of smoke and diaphanous curtains was her domain. She had been a serviceable dancer but never one that caught the eye – she belonged in the shadows where the spotlight did not shine. Without her, the dance group would have failed before they had even got started as good as they were. The same applied now. She hated Elena's shade hovering over the exquisite partnership between the Afghan and herself. Still, now as then, she realized that no one would ever witness their tormented souls glowing with brilliance within the dance movements without her. It was Caterina's last chance to be what she was born to be. She couldn't attain this fading little girl's dream without the Afghan, without Elena's machinations.

She had sat on the contact, on the offer made, terrified of revealing it to Elena's controlling ways, her grasping hands but, at the same time, afraid of missing the last train to fame.

The Afghan had reopened a door she had fatalistically closed in a time when she had thought she had already achieved her prime. Age is never kind, and this was especially true for dancers. A mortal body could only take so many sprains and bruises, physically and mentally, before youthful elegance and beauty descended into a parody of what was once natural.

She saw her life as a progression of phases – stops and starts – followed by semi-controlled lurches. She poured in her energy with each stage, convincing herself that it was all in the plan. Yet, the events would swirl around her, and most of the time, she was a lost victim to fate. Then the lull, where she would have the reoccurring battle to not fall into the pit of uncaring, of unfeeling. She knew the moment of despair would not last. Lurking at the back of her mind always lay the resentment. She would open herself reluctantly to the anticipated rush of electricity that would propel her forward into another wild dash through life. It didn't matter who the new lovers were, male or female, merely the headiness of fresh experiences that were old clothes even as she revelled in trying them on. The Afghan was a break in the monotonous and precarious cycle but much more dangerous and potentially destructive. She was afraid but had to push it through to the bitter end – wherever that was.

Now she couldn't wait for him to come back to her, to continue on her mad ride across the dance floor of her destiny.

CHAPTER X

The camp was brutal, but he was past caring. They drove them like work donkeys. Worse, one had to care for donkeys to get their labour. Every day one after the other. And, of course, it cost money to buy another beast of burden. They, on the other hand, were expendable. If you become severely injured, you are taken somewhere and dumped. It didn't matter how much you talked or to whom, for none of them knew where they were. Marched over the Hindu Kush, a nightmare of heat and cold, and down the other side, they all assumed there were somewhere in Pakistan. Where in that land of besieged faith was anyone's guess. Up at dawn, your toilet a hole in the ground and the Koran for breakfast.

Every chanted word swallowed down with a whipping across bowed backs and hunched shoulders for every stutter or mistake. A tin cup of green tea then out into the dirt – crawling, running, drilling – constant. Hot metal dismantling and mantling, driven by time and insults. The noise of gunfire, live bullets whistling over your head as you worm under netting with dust in your mouth and fear in your heart. Machetes brandished to encourage your every fading endeavour. Escape is now not even a dream. Your head lies empty - only emotions of despair remain. The ruthless instructors drive you on, training you for something, but you feel worthwhile only in your worthlessness. Fodder for a purpose for which you cannot see sense. When you are too tired to move, the drugs come out, forced down your throat, a bitterness that you cannot wash away. Soon that's all you crave, for it's the only way out of the madness.

There was no one you could trust. Some were like you - others were victims, a willing sacrifice to their faith. It was hard to tell who was who, what went on behind a man's eyes when he looked at you. Speak the wrong word, and the mark of Cain fell on you – culled in the absolute darkness of night, forgotten.

He had made it to Helmand in the end – tossed around in the back of a truck filled with sheep. He imagined himself telling Jasmine this tale in that lazy lull that overtakes your waking before duty chases you from your bed. One remembers their dreams best here, and he could see her smile as clear as daylight. This nightmare was no dream, and Jasmine was the secret that kept him alive. He followed her every move throughout his everyday existence, and he would speak to her often, holding on to the echoes of her words, too faint for him to hear but so potent that his tears would crease the dust coating his face. In his world, no one could tell the difference between sweat and tears, so Allah spared him further torment.

Helmand province was a place of rough harshness, rustic beauty and splendour. For some reason, its essence stuck deeply in him, whereas the rest of his enforced journey was a blur of turmoil and displacement. The reason for this he was never sure. Maybe it was because it was his intended journey's end. Perhaps, it was the last link with Jasmine. It was from here, at her cousin's, they had meant to reunite their normality. It never happened.

The sunsets as the burning sun fell behind the stark mountains rising from the dusty plains of Helmand had arrested him from his fall into an irretrievable place. One particular memory had staked itself into his brain, and he knew that nothing that life did to him after that would ever pull it out.

They had dragged him roughly over the truck's metal tailgate one late afternoon, banging his knees painfully and leaving bruised shins oozing blood mixed with clear fluid that had made him limp for days after. Thrown onto the broken, rocky ground, he had curled up, lost to hope, and had become mesmerised by the otherworldly scene unfolded in front of his eyes. His land of birth was majestic but what held his mind was the vision of his beautiful wife beaconing to him as she danced above the mountain peaks surrounded by the glorious reds and oranges of the setting sun. Profound loneliness had held him fast, locking his traumatized mind in a vision where his torturers could not reach.

They had long removed whatever possible mechanism he might have used to reconnect with the world from which they had torn him. At least until they had transformed him into whatever it was their twisted imaginations had in store for him. He had given up any expectation of ever seeing his beloved wife again, the only person whom he had truly loved and who returned the emotion with equal strength. He knew this unquestionably. He didn't have to examine its efficacy as many men did when times were difficult. He may have doubted many things, but not that, never. It was as automatic and relevant as every breath that he took.

He was a man castrated by fate and the ill intent of damaged men. Not just against him but against their perception of all the wrongs done to them. In the old Koranic revenge rallying call of an eye for an eye, a tooth for a tooth, they remain fixed on removing all obstacles to their objective, no matter the suffering caused to the innocent who did not share their vision of the future. The deaths of those recruited against their will were just a means to a preeminent end, justifiable retribution, even holy sacrifice. The sad truth was that in their blindness, they could not see even if they wanted to. Those they struggled against were just like them, mired in ideologies that gave the right to might – a world without end, forever and ever. 'Ameen.'

Abdul's thoughts were no longer coherent. Just a drifting of impressions and feelings that washed through his injured psyche. He was a man who leaked everywhere, no matter how much he tried to hold on to the essence of who he was. On some days, he even had difficulty remembering who he used to be.

He could see no empathy in the eyes of those who controlled his every movement. Sometimes he saw them as wild animals, for when rabid faith has pushed out any semblance of reason, there is nothing left but savagery beyond human understanding. These people who had nothing on their minds but holy revenge were outcast, shunned and feared by the very people whose interests they claimed to represent. It is that old conundrum. If you fight too hard for what you want, you lose what you have. Even among animals, the view of them would be that of an aberration.

All in all, most men merely desire to be left alone to carry out their lives. Yes, within their home's four walls, they talk up a storm – nationhood, independence, corruption, outsiders, and bloody foreigners. However, with morning's light, they get up and carry on as they always did.

This assumption was valid for Abdul, so he thought that, indeed, it applied to others in equal measure. Only when overzealous men tear down the mud bricks that protect them from the vagaries of outside political and religious fervour are they forced to rise from the bed of normality, sometimes joining the ranks of the unreasonable aggressors for want of an alternative course.

Abdul had no aggression in his heart. No ambition to propel him to pursue great things. No hate or resentment towards others. He wanted home and family, mainly his Jasmine, and the freedom to be left alone. His soul was gradually being destroyed, denied this simple aim, shrinking ever deeper within his bony chest.

Besides the warm visions of Jasmine, which were becoming dangerously close to hallucinations, the memory of the old farmer kept him anchored, not in reality but to the will to continue living.

As they had herded him over the forgotten sheep tracks and dizzying narrow trails of the forbidding Hindu Kush, it was the thought of this tough old goat of a man that kept him going. The mountains soaring majesty lorded over him, indifferent to his blistered feet and aching limbs, but this suffering brought back the hinted at farmer's earlier smuggler's life. He became his secret companion and guide. 'If I did it, sonny, so can you, eh?' His toothless grin encouraging him over the sliding, burning stones that twisted under his every step and through the summit's nerve numbing icy and frigid winds. He did not think of his dead father, his mother, his store or even his once admired father-in-law but did not consider it strange, for these memories no longer had relevance for him. He also did not pray to Allah as he once did, as these wild men, using the one God's name in such a false manner, had destroyed the intimate imagery that once resided in his heart. To him, Allah's just laws that governed social interaction and governance through the ages lay made a mockery in their crooked hands, deformed, hijacked. They claimed that the only acceptable path to the bosom of Abraham's God was through them. They were the sons of Allah and his guards. 'If they only dared,' he thought. 'They would proclaim themselves divine angels, the messengers of Allah.'

They, foreigners seeking world dominion, clash continuously with desperate, sometimes misguided sons of the soil, turning beautiful Afghanistan into a sandpit of guns, bullets and blood. Now, the people of this land is among the poorest in the world. The young, especially the men, are fleeing this life of war and discord in droves, searching for normalcy in the homelands of previous invaders. Maybe he should do the same, for these people were preparing him as a lamb for slaughter in the name of their violent cause. Had not Abraham's story taught them anything? He had to run or die beneath an explosive vest, unknown and vilified.

A decision is not sudden. It creeps up on you from every corner until all you can see is this one point of action. And so it was for Abdul. Once he saw his course, he gave it all the concentration he had left.

Abdul was a watcher and had always been like this. He took things in even when others thought that he had not understood the impact. Weeks, months, sometimes years later, Abdul would pull these experiences from wherever he had stored them and mulled them over, formulating his opinion. As then so as now, he observed. Allowing himself to be pushed, pulled and dominated in every conceivable way, but underneath his pain and indignity, Abdul studied his abusers and their movements.

He was not a man gifted with brute strength, but Allah had given him great stamina. He drew energy from a deep well, and when this well seemed to draw empty, he would dig a little further. So far, he had never been left unrewarded.

He persevered, biding his time. In the end, it was easier to slip away than he had thought. In the dark of night, there were no guards. Why bother? Who in their right mind, exhausted and abused, friendless and half-starved, would be brave or foolish enough to wander about in such a harsh and unforgiving countryside with potential harm waiting to visit upon them from every quarter. And if they did? Who cared? Replacements were a dime a dozen, as the Americans would say.

Abdul had nothing to lose as even his life counted for little. Creeping away when all others snored, he, by feel, worked his way to the dirty hut that served as a kitchen and stole stale bread, a few tins of beans and, more importantly, a bottle of water. Not wanting to exhaust the little luck he had, he scuttled off, following the stars as the old farmer had taught him during their slow, rambling, nighttime conversations.

Stars or not, he soon became hopelessly lost, but his little lucky spirit had decided not to abandon him. On the horizon, he spotted a slight sheen of light smudging the sky and headed towards it. He should have known. His perverted and sadistic instructors would not have wanted to be too far away from modern comforts despite their claims to the contrary – they were hypocrites, to their faith and cause.

It chimed midday before he staggered into the small, rural town, just a little larger than a village. At first, he thought that he walked unnoticed, but in reality, every meandering step he made lay tracked and followed by the close-knit inhabitants, many of whom stood related in one way or another. They knew well from where he had come and what his purpose was, for they had no love of the clandestine camp crouching on their borders nor for the unwelcomed fanatics that operated there within. These outsiders who opposed the rule and the law that governed their daily lives were dangerous. They invited potential retribution from the infidel dogs of war, which would ensnare their livelihoods were they ever discovered. The townsfolk knew a runaway when they saw one.

Abdul came to the alcove of a doorway and could go no further. Feeling drained right down to his bones, marrowless, he huddled on the stoop seeking surcease from the relentless heat. Having escaped the clutches of men bent on his destruction, both life and faith, Abdul slumped dejected, hoping to osmose his way out of this agony, this waiting place between the dead and the living. He had no idea of where or what to do next. The sleep of sheer exhaustion beckoned him.

'As-salaam 'Alaykum.'

His eyes flew open like a bird falling from its perch, and a polite upbringing pushed the response automatically from his cracked lips.

'Wa Alaycum As-salaam.'

Through rummy eyes gummy with infection, he tried to focus on the three men silhouetted in front of the glaring light, their shadows falling on him like a judgement from Allah.

Had his tormenters discovered him already? He felt his heart thudding madly against his bony ribs and tried to still the panic that threatened to loosen his bowels empty as they were.

Still, something was not right. These men were far too gentle. His former captives were never like this. Screaming in your face with spiteful spittle spraying was more their style of discourse.

'Are you well, young man? Are you in trouble?' came a soft voice, filled with genuine concern.

'I have committed a terrible sin, for the light of Allah has deserted me,' whispered Abdul, his dry throat hoarse and at the point of breaking.

'Are you a fugitive from the camp of the rebellious brothers, those following a path unmade by Allah?'

Abdul nodded.

'They took me against my will through the trickery of an evil-eyed truck driver. I ran away.'

'Come with us, young man. They will soon come looking for you. If they find you here, we will all be in trouble. So we prefer to avoid discord. My name is Faizan. I am the mullah in this small town of ours.'

'Don't hand me back to them. Kill me first, I beg you.'

'Come with us. We will not throw you into the hyena's den.'

Abdul did not have a choice. He could not run anymore in the state in which he was.

As good and kind as they were, the holy men had a primary concern for the welfare of their community and getting him far away was their objective.

Bundling him into the back of a battered Toyota pick-up truck, they drove him helter-skelter out of town. He had no idea where they were taking him, he hadn't asked, and they hadn't bothered to say. He felt himself beginning the process of letting go. He decided that if he wasn't inside his body and eventually, inside his mind, then anything done to him was of little consequence — what he couldn't feel couldn't hurt. He promptly fell asleep despite being bounced about like a ragged doll. He felt no anxiety about what may await him when he woke, for being asleep and awake were all the same.

When the truck came to a sudden stop, the jolt forced his eyes open, his fogged mind trying to hold on to the wisp of a tune — it sounded Afghan or was it Spanish?

In the warm yellows and salmon pinks of the setting sun, the shades of rows upon rows of tethered tents lay flapping in the dry, thin winds blowing down through the Khyber Pass. Abdul immediately knew where he was. It wasn't home, but at least he was among his people in the Khyber Pakhtunkhwa. In one of the refugee camps for his kind fleeing the scourging from war, corruption and persecution.

Without a word, the mullah nodded to him and sped off in his Toyota, leaving him standing alone on a vast dusty plain.

The words from Psalm 23:4 smoked out from a hidden niche somewhere in his memory when times were innocent and much more kind.

'Even though I walk through the shadow of the valley of death, I will fear no evil, for you are with me....'

For his everlasting shame, the image that came into his mind was not the all-merciful hand of Allah but the beautiful face of Jasmine.

'I will see you again before I die, my love, my life, even though my mind is broken to pieces by my suffering.'

The wind blew away his words, carrying them away in an eddy of dust, laughing at him. The futility of humanity's promises to itself knew no end, and he felt the mockery of the old proverb – 'Be careful what you wish, for it might come true.' When your existence depends on a wish, then indeed you are lost in the realms of illusion.

CHAPTER XI

'We are here to see Dr Mamuud Mohammad.'

There was a pause on the other side of the external intercom.

'Your name, please?' came finally an unwelcoming voice, disembodied and officious.

'We are his daughter Jasmine Abdali and his wife, Mrs Aisha Mohammad.'

'Your surname is different?'

'I am a married woman.'

'One moment, please.'

Then after a short wait with the traffic buzzing behind them, giving the feeling of being watched by curious eyes, the unfriendly voice returned.

'Do you have an appointment?'

'Yes, at three o'clock.'

'You are early. I'm afraid you'll have to return at three.'

'It says here on our appointment papers that we had to arrive fifteen minutes early to facilitate security checks.'

'You'll have to come back at three. We won't open the door until then.'

'Very well. If we are late, you will be held responsible.'

'Come back at three.'

With a muted electronic click, the intercom went dead.

'What shall we do, Jasmine?' asked her mother. Her usual confident face, worn and fearful.

'We come back at three.'

They walked around for fifteen minutes feeling as if whispers were following them – the fallen family. 'Now they know what it is like to be a nobody. Serves them right!'

At two minutes to the named hour, they pressed the intercom's metal finger smudged button once more.

'Yes!'

'We have an appointment to see Dr Mamuud Mohammad.'

'You again! I told you at three!'

'It is two minutes to three.'

'Wait a minute, please.'

Another delay, the minutes, ticking by.

'There is no one held here by that name. You'll have to enquire at the offices of the Central Prison Directorate.'

'Our papers carry their stamp. Maybe you should recheck your list.'

'I'm sorry. We can't let you in.'

'I'll like your name, please. We intend to report this outrage to the Independent Human Rights Commission.'

Once again, the intercom went dead, and no matter how much they repressed the button, it remained so.

The two women wandered away, frustrated and bewildered—the wall of faceless bureaucracy unbroken by their best efforts.

'What shall we do, Jasmine? We haven't been able to see him since they took him. Everyone is avoiding our questions, avoiding us. What shall we do?'

'I don't know, mother. I have to think.'

'And Abdul? Any word from him?'

'No, mother. For the hundredth time.'

'I'm so worried. I don't even know what to think or even how.'

'I'm sorry, mother. I know. I don't have any answers.'

Jasmine had not experienced such powerlessness before. She belonged all her life to the privileged class. They knew the right people to make things happen, usually in their favour. Now, they had cut her off, denied a father and patron, denied a husband.

Her father might well have fallen off the ends of the earth. These prisons stood designed not only to keep people in but to keep all prying eyes out – a haven for predators. They attracted and harboured sadists of all types and descriptions disguised under the drab clothing of guards and officials. Behind the enclosed, dark walls, they carried out atrocities without accountability or consequences.

She feared for her father's safety, for on this hung the well-being of his entire family, but most of all, she was terrified of Abdul's disappearance. The last time she saw him, he was rushing away from their front door. She knew that he didn't have a proper grasp of the situation or its gravity but acted solely on the implicit trust he had in her. She loved him for the complete absence of guile or evil in him. Unfortunately, she had let him down, and this thought drove her to the edge of desperation. Somewhere he was in terrible trouble, struggling way beyond his depth and crying out for her help. She couldn't be there for him. She couldn't even help herself.

'What must we do, Jasmine?'

Her mother was unrecognizable. A once comforting figure of balance and surety in life, now broken and helpless. Her house of straw, blown down by the winds of fickle fate. The proverbial wolf was at the door.

They, the dark-suited minions of false regret, had appeared at her father's house the day after his arrest.

'Your father, the good doctor, has been implicated with those involved in widescale corruption. As a result, the courts have ordered the seizure of all his assets, this house included. We are sorry, but you will have to leave within the hour and can take nothing but your clothes with you. Is there another of your family we can take you to?'

'No, thank you,' Jasmine had responded bravely. What about my husband's home and property? Have you taken that as well?'

'No, you cannot go there. Regrettably, it is also under a court order. Unfortunately, we cannot locate your husband to explain these new developments. Can you tell us where he is?'

'No, I cannot,' she had responded with bravado. 'I have no idea where my husband is. I was hoping that you could tell me.'

They had studied her with the hard stare that men of authority had used on women for time immemorial to dominate them and break their spirits.

'No, we don't, but we soon shall.'

And that was that. The good doctor's family were homeless in the blink of an eye. But, thank Allah, they were not yet destitute and had few friends and family left outside of Kabul. All those within had long since fled – rats abandoning sinking ships came to mind. However, before even thinking of making a strategic departure, they had to find her father. The lawyer, supposed family friend, they had hired was next to useless, and they had not yet had the time to locate another. Hopefully, not one who lay buried deep in the pockets of corrupt and self-interest politicians.

Every day, sometimes twice, she rang her cousin in Lashkar Gah.

'Have you seen, Abdul? Is he there?'

The answer so far had always been 'No, not a sign.'

She had to keep it together, concentrate. Otherwise, her very mind would collapse like sludge into the mud, washed away by a river of despair and anxiety.

For now, under the resentful and accusatory gazes of Abdul's mother and aunt, they squatted on their floor. It was unbearable and basic, and they were paying a handsome rent price for the questionable shelter and privilege. Her father's sister was one of those already scarpered into the night. Still, it was a necessary evil, for now, squatting with these two vultures. She and her mother had things to sort out. In the meantime, all she could do was hope and pray for Abdul.

The days crawled by as they awaited a new appointment and the relevant documents to access her father. Only Allah knew what roadblocks the prison authorities would throw up to obstruct them. Still, this time, they had managed to enlist the help of some of the doctor's old associates who sensed some political advantage in advancing their cause – scratch my back, and I will scratch yours. In reality, she really didn't care about the niceties anymore. Whatever worked gave her a degree of satisfaction.

She had made several enquiries, trying to put herself in Abdul's shoes, to think as he would. But, at the same time, she had to be cautious, for she didn't want the authorities to use her to carry through their dirty work. Handing Abdul over into their hands was the last thing she wanted.

Abdul was naïve, but he was far from stupid. Avoiding trains and planes would be high on his list. Instead, he would take his chances on the intercity busses making several intentionally separate trips rather than one long one. She was sure of that. However, checking with the bus companies was useless as record-keeping was infamously lax. Once cash was in their hands, they couldn't care less who travelled, and receipts given was wishful thinking.

Armed with a photo of Abdul, she made her way to the bus depot and made a nuisance of herself, questioning ticket clerks and bus drivers alike. Sometimes she spent all day there checking on all the departures and arrivals. Drawing several blanks did not discourage her, for she expected that.

Persistence, in the end, paid off. This luck was mainly due to Malik. Hearing about the ill fortune of his patron, he had gone out of his way to seek out Jasmine. Despite the way she had treated him, Malik was a faithful and generous soul who never seemed to bear a grudge. He also felt somewhat responsible for his wife's spiteful gossip and was determined to make amends to the Muhammad family.

Malik was a man who knew everyone and was universally loved by all. He had many cousins who drove buses, and he would meet Jasmine at the bus station every morning to accompany her. This gesture covered two necessities. First, he provided a male chaperon that every respectable married Muslim woman required, and, second, he presented an opening to many helpful contacts.

By chance, after a morning of disappointment, a young, thin driver of Pashtun ethnicity hailed Malik loudly. He was indebted to the resourceful man for many undeclared favours done in the past and wanted to show his goodwill.

'Malik! Malik!' he yelled, his head bobbing up and down over the milling crowd.

The spindly-legged driver dodged nimbly through the busy throng and hugged Malik to Jasmine's surprise, kissing him on both cheeks whilst laughing with delight.

'Stop that!' responded Malik gruffly, holding the fellow from him at arm's length, but he had a twinkle in his eye.

Then turning his head to look at Jasmine, Malik said.

'This overly affectionate rascal has managed to get himself married to my baby sister. Whatever you do, don't trust him. He's as slippery as an eel.'

The so-named rascal immediately disengaged himself from Malik's grasp and, placing his hand over his heart, nodded to Jasmine.

'Mukhtar, this is the daughter of Dr Muhammad. She is looking for her husband. Look at this picture. Have you seen him?'

Studying the photo with an intense frown, Mukhtar, now grave and unsmiling, nodded again.

'Yes, I think so. Yes, I remember this face. He looked like a lost boy, clutching a bag to his chest as if it would protect him. I'm sorry. I had no idea who he was. That was a bad trip.'

'Why do you say that, Mukhtar?' asked Malik.

'Fat Azzat is getting more and more greedy. If I had known he was manning the highway checkpoint, I'd have stayed in bed. Begging your pardon, but your husband didn't seem to know the rules. He didn't have a bribe ready for Fat Azzat.'

'My husband is a good man with a pure heart, but he does not always see the things he should. What happened, and who is Fat Azzat?'

'A pig. A greedy good for nothing swine whose rich uncle bought him a commission as a lieutenant in the police force. He is a coward and a bully. A dangerous predator.'

'Careful, Mukhtar. You will cause Mrs Jasmine to over-worry,' cautioned Malik. 'Tell us what happened.'

'Fat Azzat saw your husband hugging his bag like a baby, hugs his pillow and demanded to see it. I thought he was going to shoot the poor bugger there and then. Sorry, ma'am. Thank Allah he only grabbed the bag but what he saw inside made him sweat like an old horse in the midday sun. He tried to force your husband to get off the bus, but the Americans arrived and put the fear of a hot poker up him. That was that. I drove out of there as fast as I could.'

'With my husband on board, I hope,' responded Jasmine fiercely.

'Yes, ma'am.'

'Do you recall where he got off,' she asked.

'At Jalalabad. He scuttled off like a crab under a fisherman's hand, trying to crane his neck in every direction at once—the poor devil. I didn't pay any further notice after he stepped off my bus. He brought bad luck with him, I'm afraid.'

'Mukhtar, remember to whom you're talking. Show some respect!' chastised Malik.

'Sorry, Mrs Muhammad. I get carried away sometimes.'

'Abdali. My name is Abdali. My husband's name.'

'Sorry, Mrs Abdali. I mean no offence,' replied a chagrined Mukhtar.

Nodding her head, Jasmine turned and walked away, her eyes glazed and distant.

'Thank you, Mukhtar. We'll be expecting you for tea when your shift finishes,' she could hear Malik talking to Mukhtar. She didn't care one bit whether she was rude or not. Her loving husband was somewhere out there in her torn land without money, with unknown people chasing him and no friends or family in his sight.

Jasmine accepted that nothing remained for her to do. She was worse off for knowing than not knowing. Initially, she felt secure that Abdul could buy his way out of any problematic situation with the money he had on his person. Yes, he seemed to be taking his time about it, but eventually, he would turn up at Lashkar Gah and her cousin's. Now, however, it was beyond doubt that he stood lost in a world of trouble. Thanks to this odious sounding Fat Azzat. Someone had long thrown her country to the dogs, and the curs were growing bloated on their suffering. All that fate had left her was the agony of patience and the futility of prayers.

She threw all her fury and anger into chasing the shifty, faceless bureaucrats who hid their duplicitous intentions behind laws and regulations. By now, their fast-depleting funds, deposited and squirrelled away in bank accounts in her and her mother's name, in hindsight a reasonable safety precaution, had bought them a team of clever lawyers. Standing behind these legal prostitutes stooped shadowy politicians, whispering into their ears. They calculated that their actions might one day buy them a place in the gaze of the overseeing Americans – a glorified whistleblower. The invaders were always looking for emotional heart-string stories – nothing better to hide reality than good publicity. Her father, the good doctor, was a prime protagonist for such fiction, and she knew it. If this subterfuge won him his freedom, then so be it. She would become an accomplice.

It wasn't long before the incarceration of Dr Muhammad baked itself into a red-hot potato – far too hot to handle for a government who wanted to concentrate on far more positive things. Taking a magnanimous u-turn, they quickly expedited the release of the doctor, taking the public stance that he had always been a man for the people despite him being somewhat misguided. Unfortunately, the price of his freedom was the seizure of all his money, businesses and assets, which they would use towards financing Afghan refugee camps abroad – 'Until our displaced citizens, sons of Afghanistan, come safely home.' What a humanitarian declaration but no mention of the daughters.

'Hypocrites! All of them!' thought Jasmine.

Privately, the Muhammad family was summarily stripped of all rights and citizenship with the choice of exile or face poverty and constant harassment.

The decision was simple. However, there was still milk to be squeezed from the udder of the doctor and his family's story.

The well-educated and clever spin doctors got to work and hashed out an agreement for political asylum – an ace card to be hidden in the pack for a possible future gambit.

The Muhammad family would fly to America. The sooner, the better for all concerned except, of course, for Jasmine. She had a missing husband to find.

CHAPTER XII

Her heart was thudding wildly in her chest, on a level way down in her belly. She wasn't a guileless teenager, a victim of the unstoppable surging of novel hormones. She was a grown woman, a veteran of many conquests. Yet her body was responding, reacting, in a fashion that left her incapacitated, helpless, and gasping.

It wasn't merely a sexual possession, but something more. An orgasm before the physical act even started. It was a Damascus moment, spiritual and overwhelming, sucked down a narrow tunnel to unconditional release – a road to fulfilling her art and talent.

She had to pull herself back from panting into his ears as he shuffled past, oblivious to her heightened state of arousal. Instead, she planted a quick kiss on his cheek.

'Go and run yourself a cold shower, dear,' Elena chuckled, unable to resist a spiteful dig.

Caterina hated her.

She took in a deep breath and tried to douse the rising heat between her thighs.

'Have you got anything for me?' continued Elena, the mocking tone still coursing through her voice. 'Or have you been merely wasting your time on your back daydreaming of other things? They say it makes you blind, you know.'

Caterina hated her even more, but the bitch had a point. Her thoughts were all over the place—a malady of the mentally blind.

'Yeah, I've got something for you alright – a number,' she heard herself saying. 'It's your last chance, so don't waste it.'

She felt a cheap satisfaction with the surprise and puzzlement written loud in her old lover's eyes.

'A number?'

'That's what I said, mi querida. Unfortunately, the wrinkles are not the only sign, I see.'

To give her credit where it was due, Elena broke into peals of genuine laughter.

'Touché!' she chuckled. 'Those claws again? Pull them in, sweet girl. Now,

what are you talking about? What number? Tell me all, my dearest.'
'An agency rang. I recognized their name. They have a reputation for
getting their clients noticed. So I said we'd call them back.'
'I knew it! I said it would happen!' squealed Elena. 'Good girl! You're a
darling! Please give me that number, mi querida. The big times are calling!'
   Elena's sudden explosive joy was infectious, and despite herself, Caterina
returned her tight hug, laughing with her. They did not see the Afghan
regarding them, his face expressionless but his black eyes glittering with
disdain. It was the only emotion he had ever revealed, and the two
celebrants remained unaware of it.
   Something about the attitudes of these women had called Abdul from
where he hid back to the surface. All be it briefly. They reminded him of
the mother and aunt he had long forgotten. A patterned carpet – the centre
of personal gain and self-serving interest. The smell of nuts, heavy in the
heated air. He retreated swiftly to the darkness within his mind.
   Elena didn't waste any time.
'Look, Caterina,' she said. 'This is serious now. I need your authorization to
speak with confidence with these people. Any chance they get, they will
take us for a ride.'
'What do you need?' responded Caterina, her natural suspicions of Elena's
intentions taking a back seat to her lifelong dream's aspirations.
'I need you to make my position legal. That means signing some papers.'
'What about the Afghan? He has rights as well.'
'Of course, he does. But does he look as if he cares one way or another?'
said Elena, her tone dismissive and cynical. 'I'll draw up some papers for
both of you to sign. I'm sure we can coax him to make his mark. Do you
know whether or not he can even read or write English?'
   Neither woman bothered to look at or even glance at the man they were so
blithely discussing. They had already come to the unilateral position that his
opinion did not matter even if he heard or understood.
   After a short pause of recollection, Caterina shook her head.
'No. I have no idea.'
'There you have it then. We'll speak for the Afghan and decide in his best
interest. I'll arrange it so that we become his Power of Attorney and make
decisions on his behalf.'
'Can you do that? Is it legal?' asked Caterina.
'Of course, it is, dear. All we need are a couple of witnesses. After all, if we
don't do this, the agents will usurp his rights, and we can't have that, can
we?'
   Caterina frowned but didn't answer.
'Leave it to me, mi querida. I'll sort it all out. Don't worry your pretty head.
Your job is to concentrate on the next show. You'll have to do something
even better than you did before. It's time to really impress. Forward that

number to me. I'll make the calls tonight. Take care of our friend there. See if you can get him to drink less. Can't have him dying on us before we even get started.'

Caterina couldn't wait for Elena to leave. The euphoria ignited by the good news had her chatting as she used to do in the old days. However, Caterina did not desire those times back. She had moved on. All she wanted was for Elena to go so that she could share her excitement with the Afghan – get him somehow to feel what she was feeling.

Eventually, she managed to usher Elena out under the pretext that she had to start seriously planning for the next event and try it out on the Afghan. Elena was much too preoccupied with dollar signs to recognize the little subterfuge and left promising to call back later with the new developments.

Caterina sensed the subtle difference as soon as she sat next to the Afghan. It wasn't a physical thing, for, as usual, he did not react to her presence or move one centimetre. But there was something – a withdrawal of sorts. She couldn't put her finger on it and say, 'There it is!' It was invisible, a psychic shift in the air, a change in the atmosphere.

Inexplicably, panic took hold of her, and she reached out to him, grabbing at him desperately and pulling his unresponsive body close, trying to detect the undetectable through the warmth of touch – the melding of flesh to flesh. A lost feeling of being too late overcame her, and she felt the yawning of the void reaching out to swallow her. She did not want to surrender to that black place – not now.

There was a grey space, fading in and out like a faint harbinger of hope in a storm-filled sky. But, the black clouds lay thick all around, and it was safer to stay hidden, for the grey was a false sign of light—an illusion haloed by suspicion. To struggle towards it was only to invite the waiting presence of disappointment and pain. Bright dawn belonged to stories that have long faded, slipped away into nothingness – neither a beginning nor an end.

Whenever the music played, visions of Jasmine, raven-haired and sparkling eyes of emerald green, reached in and led him out. Whenever he followed her through, stepping into the open, she changed, morphing into someone else. Still, her image as she once existed burned on in his mind. He no longer knew what was real and what was a mirage. So, he joined in the dance to hold on to her. As the image dissolved, like a mist, he danced the more, his only lifeline to a beautiful time - or was it just a dream? Something that only took form in the inky blackness of memories to keep him from tumbling entirely into the abyss of insanity.

Sometimes he glimpsed the woman who danced in Jasmine's shoes. He felt the passion steaming from her overheated body as it swirled in a sensual haze around him, trying to seize him, keep him in place, and stop him from retreating.

She was always watching, lying in ambush like a predatory succubus, the incarnate of Lilleth, coaxing him with the secret music that belonged to him and Jasmine – a trickster. But, against his better judgment, he would nearly always fall for her wiles, clothed as she was in the guise of his wife's beauty. Then she would pounce on him like a panther in season, claws sharp, pinning him under her arousal, tearing from him what was not hers to have.

He knew that he was partly to blame. He had an unpardonable weakness – a willingness, need even, to recreate the likeness of his Jasmine and implant it into any female vessel that showed him her interest. Was he delusional or simply a thief perverting the trust his marriage demanded of him? Was he merely giving in to his carnal desires under pretentious excuses?

He dimly remembered a blond-haired woman and a little girl with eyes of blue peeking out from behind her dress. The flashback caused him pain, and he immediately dismissed it, pushing it back out of sight. Every action, even inaction, has consequences. He had used these two for his comfort, discarding them when they became inconvenient for his selfishly hoarded agony – self-flagellation brings forth righteousness. Did that make him a predator or victim of life? He was a member of the underserved, and this is why Allah continually punishes him. Was his wife's pure saintly image held like a shield in his heart, a reflection of his guilt and failure as a man, a husband? After all, he had run from her like a coward, deserting her when she needed him most—abandoned to face adversarial uncertainties on her own – a woman without her husband's protection in a patriarchal world of guns, religion and politics. He had not even made an acceptable effort to find out what had become of her, trusting that her well-connected family stood better placed to shelter her – an opt-out before the gaze of Allah, of marital responsibility.

This woman whom he remotely felt clutching at him frightened him. She mirrored his inner demons with her own – frail but at the same time fierce and unpredictable. She dug into his entrails relentlessly, trying to drag out that part of him that attracted and obsessed her – the dance he danced with Jasmine. It was not hers to have, but she coveted it, exploited it, and sucked on it to feed her talent. He did not want her to have this inner part of him, but his hallucinations confused his reality to such an extent that he yearned slavishly for the illusion of reality that remained in his power to make. Even if his balming efforts were merely a simulacrum of his Jasmine, they were both culpable – the yin and yang of selfish desire.

Caterina could not see this cauldron of cyclical turmoil roiling with futility within the soul of Abdul. She sensed, however, that he wasn't as disconnected from the world as she had hitherto thought. Was he hiding and watching - observing their usage and manipulation of him to fulfil their unachieved dreams? She certainly felt a withdrawal. Was it from disapproval of their intent? It made her uneasy, but most of all, she was fearful of losing the little she had of him – like water trickling through her fingers, the more her grip tightened, the more she lost.

Yes, he was integral to gaining those heights that had eluded her all her life, but she envisioned him riding high with her at the finishing line. He wasn't just a means to an end. He was part of the cherry pie of their success, and she wanted him with her all the way.

She took hold of his face with her long slender fingers and turned his head, forcing him to give some degree of eye contact. His black eyes were like vacant bottomless pools, and when she looked into them, she started to lose her path.

'You can't fool me,' she whispered. 'I know you're in there, and I know you can hear me. I want you to trust me. I won't betray you, but we have to be careful, for she will.'

She thought she saw something swim past in the empty pool, but maybe because she wished it so much.

It was vital for her to reach this man, link with him, form a partnership. Remaining separate entities was not an option. Elena was counting on that. In this way, she could control them, eat them up to feed her ambition.

With a wistful sigh, she got up and made her way to the stereo disk player. It was time to commence the lengthy trial and error, like finding the magic numbers to open a treasure box. One music selection after the next, endless stroking and coaxing, hoping to find a spark, then gently blowing that ember into a raging flame designed to devour any audience. It wasn't a sure thing, and at the moment, it remained hit and miss—more miss than a hit to tell the truth. It terrified her that in the future, if she failed to break into the Afghan's armour, she would no longer be able to find that sweet spot. If this happened, her dreams would die, and she was terrified that she would never recover from that. Her life would lie behind her, a wasteland of almost endeavours. The failure her mother always told her she would be.

She had been making progress with the Afghan. He relied less and less on alcohol to find sleep and some healing with luck. He showered without prompting and took time to groom himself – well, more or less, for she enjoyed brushing his hair till it shone and shaving him was an exquisite act of concentration and intimacy. Once or twice she had even caught him looking at her as if he were trying to remember something. Admittedly, the look was fleeting, but it was a step in the right direction. Of course, she made sure never to tell Elena these things. Let the bitch continue to think that she was irreplaceable. Good managers were a dime a dozen. Well, perhaps not, but never mind.

The invasive buzzing of her mobile stuck in a draw somewhere demanded that she should come and release it, insisting that she remained connected to a frivolous and uncaring world. Instead, she surrendered as she had always done, fearful of missing something that might be important.

The voice on the other end was brimming with self-congratulations and confidence. Caterina had to fight the urge to shut it off with a touch, but at the same time, she wanted to hear the news that she knew would eventually entrap her and possibly destroy her. How easy it was to be weak, to be a victim. A victim had all the excuses and no shortages of willing ears to listen to them.

'I've got all the documents, mi querida, and a lawyer to represent us. I've also made contact with the agents, and we have an appointment next week.'

'That was fast work, Elena. It makes me think you anticipated this eventuality already. You're becoming predictable, dear.'

'Don't get paranoid on me, mi querida. A second dose of stage fright is the last thing we need right now. We're too old for a third chance, aren't we, dearest?'

Caterina wasn't surprised in the least by her friend's preparedness. She was a vulture and couldn't change her nature.

She worked tirelessly with the Afghan throughout the intervening days, but her efforts were so far fruitless. His hidden self emerged a few times, and they danced through old flames, but she was no longer satisfied with that. She wanted an inferno.

The day of the meeting arrived all too quickly, and true to her habits, Elena showed up early with the legal papers. With her strolled a lawyer who went about his business in a brisk but surly manner. Tagging on behind them was one of the young Latino toughs from her bar who broadly grinned when he spotted the Afghan. This greeting, open as it was, went unanswered, but the bouncer seemed unfaced, for he remembered well the timed intervention that, without doubt, had saved his life. In his culture, debt was a debt, and repayment was obligatory. Besides, the Afghan's recent exploits were the talk of the community, and he enjoyed the associated local fame of being a familiar.

To Elena's finger tapping impatience, Caterina took the time to explain the procedure to a seemingly uncaring Afghan, but her conscience would not allow her to do anything less. When she finished, she invited him to sign with a pointed finger, and they were all taken aback by his precise and flowing signature.

'Has he had a psychological assessment?' asked the lawyer, frowning at the Afghan.

'Never you mind that!' replied an acerbic Elena. 'Besides, haven't I paid you enough? Look at him, man, are you blind as well as stupid!'

The lawyer did as she had compensated him for doing, and the procedure was painlessly short if questionable.

In addition to her insufferable self, Elena now took on the over-the-top airs and graces of an entitled prima-donna. This appropriation made her even more unbearable to be around. She dismissed the swell-headed lawyer and her roguish employee with a hand wave of superb condescension. After they had left wordlessly, she spent a few minutes packing away the signed papers in a leather case, done with an excessive flourish.

'Time to go, my flowers. Our destiny awaits.'

Taking the Afghan by the hand, Caterina followed her out the door.

They arrived early at the plush offices of the music agent and announced themselves, or rather, Elena did. The receptionist flashed them a white-toothed painted smile as they entered and bid them sit in comfort while waiting for the appointment.

Fixing the receptionist with a cold stare, Elena calmly replied.

'Your people asked to see us, not the other way round. So if they cannot show the courtesy of seeing us now, we'll be on our way.'

'Ah, please be seated. I'll go and let my employers know that you're here early.'

Elena gave the receptionist a perfunctory nod then turned away.

As the flustered greeter and meeter disappeared through a plain white door across the hall, Elena turned to Caterina and winked.

'Start as we mean to go on, eh? So we can't let them get the upper hand. Bad for business.'

No one could take it away from her. The woman had the nerve and balls to boot.

Caterina couldn't help but smile.

It didn't take long for the agent to come rushing out, displaying a full armour of smiles and apologies.

'That's a good sign,' thought Caterina. 'We must have made quite a mark. Enough for these money speculators to think that they could make a buck or two off our backs.'

The agent kicked off the meeting with lots of pleasantries, congratulations and how impressed she was with the dynamism and vibrancy of Caterina and the Afghan's performances. She was there among the crowds at the street corners from the beginning, she said. She had been bowled over by how the spectators had been captivated and enthralled. They were raw, yes. They needed a bit of sophistication, yes, but she could supply that, and she had in mind the ideal exposure for them.

Moreover, she had the connections to a venue that would launch them into the eyes of a large audience on a national scale. Her choreographers would be able to do wonders for them. All that was necessary was for them to put themselves into her capable hands. Then, their worries were all but over.

'They are already in capable hands, dear,' interjected Elena. 'And there is no one better at choreographing than Caterina. I'm sure you must have heard of the dance company called 'Not just Flamenco?'

'Erh, I'm not sure that I have.'

'Don't let's play games, mi querida. I've done my research. I recall, you guys were knocking clamorously on the door at the time, shouting for a slice of the party cake.'

'Oh, yes. I do remember now,' replied the agent smugly. 'The company went bust, didn't they?'

'Not exactly, and you know it. My people had the choice of much bigger contracts than you were offering, in which, I might add, the choreographer and star dancer, Caterina here, was an integral part of any deal.'

The agent relaxed back into her chair and fixed Elena with a flinty business eye.

'You haven't changed much from those times, I see. So what is it you're suggesting?'

'Oh, isn't it nice to be remembered fondly,' purred Elena. 'Now, we can stop the bull-shit and discuss what matters really. We decline your generous offer of choreographing. Our level of sophistication depends on the status of the venues you can present to us. Any other management in that quarter is unnecessary. We will leave the acquisition of all platforms entirely in your hands and are happy to allow you generous compensation for your efforts. However, if our performances do not generate the expected audience, we will step away, voiding the contract but meeting your up-front expenses.'

'Bullish as ever, but your broad terms are agreeable. But, of course, we will still have to discuss the finer points and exactly what you mean by generous compensation,' responded the agent.

'I'm happy to enter those discussions at any time,' said Elena dismissively. 'But tell me. What was that you said earlier about an ideal exposure?'

The agent suddenly relaxed and leant forward with enthusiasm springing out of her every pore.

'Yes, yes. We've been waiting for someone like Caterina and this amazing young man to come onto our books for ages. From what we've seen, they have the skill and presence to sweep into a notable national competition that has been running on TV for two months now. It's oh so trendy and proving exceptionally popular. I must say that it has been dominating the ratings since it started.'

'You're not referring to the people versus the stars competition, are you? If you can get us on that, it would be a winner for us all!' exclaimed Elena matching the agent's excitement.

They seemed to have forgotten the presence of Caterina and the Afghan without whom nothing of what they were discussing would take place.

Irritated by being so blatantly sidelined, Caterina cut in with a voice as sharp as a knife with a serrated edge.

'Don't mind us, eh, girls. When you finish counting money and building your fame on our backs, please, inform us what is essential. Now, if you'll excuse us, we are going in search of fresh air.'

The two dancers, hand in hand, departed the room leaving behind a pocket of uncomfortable silence.

CHAPTER XIII

A person knows when he is genuinely empty, for even his tears have deserted him. His centre is a dry place where nothing lives, and there is no memory of emotion. He sees and hears but does not feel. Life has lost all flavour, and there is no joy - even pain is but a background noise, constant to the point of normality, like droning traffic. Hope is an illusion and has long been abandoned, left on the roadside somewhere in the dirt and dust.

Most of us take the comforts, food, shelter, clean water, a change of clothing, family and friends, all gone and almost forgotten for granted. A different time, a reality, perhaps, that never existed.

The overriding sensation is one of extreme tiredness. You feel fatigued on the outside. Inside, you are exhausted - too wearied to think, too tired to eat, and too spent to live. You desperately need help but don't know how to ask for it or even who to ask. Can anyone be trusted? You can't be bothered at times, for it costs too much of what you don't have or are unwilling to surrender. A person, even a nobody, must keep back something to remember who he was. Worth is a seed, not a grain of sand.

And what is hunger, after all, when you cannot last recollect when your stomach was full? If you were offered a feast today, at this moment, you would pick at the edges and chew for ages, one tiny morsel at a time, for fear of throwing up. What little dignity you still possessed, disgorged sourly for all to see and sneer.

'What is your name?'

Why is that always the first question? Asked with a certain smugness as if winning this information is the possession of your soul — conquered and put in its place.

It took a long time to answer. It was Abdul of that he was sure for that was his given name. Had he forgotten his identity? What was his father's? His grandfather? His mother even. They were all there somewhere, but he couldn't find them, lost in the numb jumble that was his mind. He would eventually, but it would take time. Did he care?

'What is your name, son? From where have you come?'

The second question was there before he could answer the first.

Left standing in the deserted, dust-blown, no man's zone outside the tall, barbed wire fencing that gave the impression of either security or imprisonment within, Abdul had little choice but to approach the closed gate. A bored-looking guard met him there, or was it the other way around? He had no recollection of the guard moving. He was just there, looking through him as if Abdul was a figment of his very own imagination – a ghost trapped in another world, dead to the one he once inhabited.

He tried to tell the guard that he wanted to go in but was unsure what his actual words were.

With a perfunctory gesture with the rifle that empowered him, the sentinel indicated that he should come back tomorrow as the camp was now closed to outsiders.

Was he a non-belonger then? Among his very own countrymen? The cold assessment and perhaps condemnation sent a cutting wind blowing through his suspended thoughts. What was the purpose of this emblem of unapproachable authority, not much older than Abdul, if that? To keep people in or deny others entry?

With nothing left to do, he sat with his back against the fence in the dirt and waited through a bitter night where even sleep fled before the icy cold. His wasted muscles shivered so violently that by morning they were locked into spasming knots. He could not move until the first rays of sun found him, thawing him out and relaxing his torment.

Consigned to feel like a stray, beaten dog with its tail tucked beneath its legs, Abdul struggled to the point where the guard had forced him to leave the evening before. By now, there were others, all bedraggled and desperate, brothers together in the name of a cause.

In this forsaken queue, he slunk to a spot behind a tall, lean man with red in his beard, holding the hand of a little girl of about seven. She asked him for water as she was thirsty and trusted in the divine capabilities of her elder, who, by the look of it, could not be anyone else but her father. He told her that she had to be strong, for there was no water. A little while later, she repeated her desire and received the same answer. Yet again, she asked, and her father knowing his position of weakness, promised her he would ask the guard, which was a different one yet the same from the night before. Glancing at Abdul, he seemed to implore him to keep an eye on his daughter in case of the inevitable. Straightening his thin soldiers, he advanced on the guard.

The result was as he had expected. The guard mocked him and beat him back with the butt of his rifle. Like all little girls, his daughter saw her duty to care for her father and put her little arms around him, striving her best to soothe his hurt and wounded pride.

That small pocket of love firmed the last resolve in Abdul's heart, and he stepped closer to the man and his daughter to convey his moral solidarity and lend them strength. This camp represented the legal claim of the bereft to the rights of humanity. Abdul was sure that beating a refugee for wanting water for his daughter was not legal or justifiable in any man's language.

The queue wasn't going anywhere fast, but the sun was getting higher and hotter. The little girl had long since given up the idea of ever getting water but some good person somewhere in the line handed down a broken umbrella to shelter her from the sun. Waiting was the only game within anyone's control.

It wasn't that the gate remained permanently locked. No, far from it, there was an intermittent stream of vehicles going in and out, some being expensive western made cars. They, the camp guardians, waved them through without even a cursory check.

Now and again, a window would roll down, and the lens of a camera would poke out, taking cliché photos of the dispossessed for the selling to well-meaning do-gooders to debate and donate. Their misery was the fodder for the guilt of the world. So many pointed their attention at the little girl, ignoring the patient men and women baking in the line. It was a violation of an innocent humiliated by filth, neglect, rich men's wars and ambition. This camp was here in the name of the dispossessed, but they had nothing to offer, only take, in the eyes of those who controlled their fate. As usual in this world of inequality, the wealthy donors in their expensive cars with tinted windows were desired. They were the dignitaries, the philanthropists. Without them, there would not be a camp, so they were the priority. Such is the logic and the way of things.

The gate opened by some arbitrary signal, which was not visible to the petitioners, allowing those first in line to shuffle through. Abdul, the little girl and her father, were not one of them. So they waited – sweat trickling through the dirt on their bodies.

It wasn't until well beyond noon that they let them in. By then, the little girl was silent and no longer able to stand on her feet. What became of them, Abdul had no idea, but later, he would have some suspicions. He offered up a prayer to Allah on their behalf.

As they came through the gates, they separated them. Whether to see to their needs or to weed out undesirables remained unclear – paired out and processed.

Abdul followed a woman who beckoned him imperiously. What else could he do?

She guided him into a plain wooden building that served as an administrative point of some sort. Waved into a too-short chair that wobbled on shaky legs, he sat down with an air of dejection and resignation. Come what may, he no longer cared.

A man, an Afghan by the look of him, joined the officious woman, and they took ages ignoring him with their superfluous preparations – shuffling of papers and opening and closing the draws of their desk.

'So, what's your name, son?' the man asked.

Abdul struggled to recall his mind from where it floated and think things through. It was difficult to see his way around the thick foggy heat and dust that blocked his focus.

'What's your name, son? Where have you come from?'

'Kabul,' he replied, frowning deeply in concentration.

'Ah,' said the man, scribbling on a notepad. 'And your name?'

'Abdul.'

'Ah, Abdul from Kabul. Do you have any skills – a trade?'

'Skills? No, I haven't got any.'

'I see,' said the man, followed by more writing. 'By your accent, I would say you're not a farmer. Education?'

'Eh?'

The man sighed wearily.

'Did you go to school, Abdul, and for how long?'

'Yes. University.'

'You attended Kabul University?'

The dismissive woman stopped what she was doing, whatever that was, and eyed Abdul as if he were an insect discovered crawling on her bed.

'Father?'

'What?'

'Your father, Abdul. What did he do?'

'Dead.'

'My condolences, Abdul. What was his profession?'

'He was a merchant.'

'I see. Have you married, Abdul?'

'Yes, my wife is waiting for me.'

'Ah, may Allah shine his light on her. What is her name, Abdul? Her full name.'

'Jasmine Abdali. She is the most beautiful woman in all the world.'

'Women are Allah's gift to man, and one that has beauty inside or out is the most precious. You are a fortunate man, Abdul. Is Abdali your family's name?'

Abdul nodded, his attention appearing to be drifting away.

'Abdul, what is your wife's maiden name?'

'She is the daughter of Dr Mahmoud Mohammad. They took him away. I must help them.'

The woman's loud in-suck of breath disrupted the man's careful questioning.

He regarded her with a mild look of annoyance.

'Is something wrong?' he asked softly.

'May I have a word? I recognise that name.'

'I see. Please excuse us, Abdul. We won't be long.'

Abdul did not respond. Not even with curiosity.

They were not even sure if he noticed them getting up and walking away.

After a few moments with the woman gesticulating and whispering wildly, the man calmly returned.

'Thank you for being so patient with us, Abdul. My colleague here insists that she knows of your father in law, Dr Mohammad. She says that he was a man of significant influence, wealth and government connections who they snagged in the end in an anti-corruption net. Is this true, Abdul?'

'I don't know of this corruption. What I do know is that the doctor was a good man who helped me set up an honest business with my wife. But, unfortunately, we both failed her in the end. We should have protected her, but I ran like a coward.'

'Are you a wanted man, Abdul Abdali? A fugitive? Perhaps a criminal? Are you a danger to us here? Will you be tainted honey attracting flies?'

'I don't care what you think or do. We did nothing wrong. All I want is my Jasmine. Politics is a game for the clever. I was never that.'

'I see, Abdul. I think you are one of life's innocent, or are you merely proficient at it – showing what you need to? You are more than you seem, young man. Otherwise, you would not have survived the road you have just travelled.'

'We cannot let him stay here. It will cause an incident, and we cannot afford that,' spat the woman, glaring at Abdul as if he were an infiltrator bent on doing them harm.

The soft-spoken man ignored her.

'Abdul, this camp needs people like you. Will you stay and help us?'

The woman stared at her senior colleague in shock, nonpulsed by his unforeseen words, and Abdul seemed uncomprehending.

'What can you possibly want from me?' asked Abdul. 'I have nothing to offer.'

'On the contrary, Abdul. You have education,' replied the administrator. 'This camp is filled with poor farmers and their children. You can help to give them a better future but first, let's get you settled. You will have to share a tent, I'm afraid. This camp cannot afford luxuries.'

With his registration completed, they handed Abdul a compact case of toiletries, toothpaste, toothbrush, a bar of soap, two threadbare blankets along with two cans of out of date luncheon meat and a few bags of tea. That was it. As the man said, there were no luxuries here. Nevertheless, it was more than Abdul had had for a long time.

The man called over to a skinny Afghan boy with green irises who Abdul instantly liked simply because his eye colour reminded him of Jasmine. The administrator gave the boy instructions, which Abdul could not follow and disappeared back into the building with a nod to Abdul.

The boy gestured for Abdul to follow then set off briskly through the camp, which soon became a maze of narrow paths through a city of tents filled with smells and muddy puddles. Abdul stood lost within the first ten steps and hurried to catch up to the boy.

They eventually arrived at a tent the same as others, just another brown wave in a sea of homogenous dwellings.

The boy scratched on the closed tent flap, and after a short pause, a young bearded face popped out.

'Mukteer! Why aren't you at your lessons?' was the immediate response.

The boy, named Mukteer, screwed up his face in part annoyance, part embarrassment.

'Brought you your new tent-mate, haven't I?' was the truculent reply, and with a gesture towards Abdul, he turned and fled.

'That fish is a hard one to hook,' said the bearded young man, shaking his head at Mukteer's departing back. 'You must be our new teacher. Welcome to our ranks and lodge. It's humble but comfortable. What shall we call you?'

'Abdul.'

'Come on in, Abdul. I'm the only one here at the moment - cooking rota, you see. However, two other learned gentlemen will soon join us. By the way, my name is Peter.'

'Peter?'

'Yes, yes. It's a long story. I'll fill you in during dinner.'

'Err, Peter. I'm not sure about this. No one said that I was to teach. I was never a teacher.'

'Ah, I can see that they've recruited you in the usual manner. Don't worry about it. That's the way things work around here. You'll fit in nicely.'

Peter's enthusiastic and open approach to everything reassured Abdul, and he settled down cross-legged on the hard-packed dirt floor to watch him cook on a clay pot contraption fueled by lumps of coal. Luncheon meat, it seems, was on the menu.

In the end, his fellow teachers turned out to be all easy-going young men who gave out all the signals that they were doing something worthwhile.

'Mosactoneer will take you to our classrooms and your students tomorrow, Abdul. You'll take to it like a duck to water, don't worry.'

'Peter, if you please. That name was merely my father's revenge on my mother for running away with the neighbour,' interrupted Peter.

Whether Peter was serious or not, Abdul had no idea.

And so, Abdul became a member of the small fraternity of teachers in the camp. As was the Muslim way, his students were boys. A tightly knitted group of youthful women taught the girls at a separate part of the camp, students not much younger than them. Abdul began to learn about the daily reality of where he had ended up through these lively and mischievous boys.

It was they, many of whom had sisters or cousins studying with the mirror image set up, except for their gender, in a different area of the camp or, as he was beginning to suspect, an open-air prison. They all wanted a way out. Staying in this sprawling, dangerous fenced-in purgatory with its contaminated water, expired food, limited freedom, and hardly any self-determination was a choice for survival – nothing more. They had few belongings and barely a change of clothing. In the summer, they sweltered, plagued with constant thirst and threatened by disease. In winter, they shivered under their blanket wrappings and longed for their destroyed mud-brick farmhouses, where they once experienced the warmth of family and tribal neighbours.

They were much more than outcasts. They were prey. The predators were men disguised as well-dressed donors, deep, full pockets and empty of morality, circling the helpless with intent to despoil.

The tales of these boys, many of whom had seen the worst of what war had to offer and had never experienced peace and security in their short lives, told with a frank matter of fact voice were harrowing.

These men, oiled and perfumed, bodies adorned with trinkets of gold, wanted something in return for their benevolence.

Was this the fate in waiting for the lovely, innocent and loyal little girl at the gates? Was she the final ace card her father would have to put in play to free her from this soulless confinement?

The boys told of families fitting out their young daughters in bright blue dresses and surrendering them into the shaky hands of unverified suitors as their last hope for her liberation and, by extension, theirs. It was not profiteering from bridal exchanges, nor did they mean to be cruel. These were traditional tribal families who believed in and had faith in the marriage laws of Allah. However, like their boys, their girls had also lived with war and its ravages. Heartless abuse runs unchecked with violators who seek power, control, revenge and a deposit in which to empty their rage. The poor, the marginalized, the helpless, and women, many still girls clutching dolls, are the first to fall. The shame is all-consuming in a culture where the intact hymen is a holy offering in marriage. The sole avenue available to hide this humiliation is to find a giving, caring husband for their ruptured daughters. The constant danger was that such baseless men would marry a girl and not pay the dowry, only to divorce and abandon her a week or so later. Marriage provided a religiously permissible cover for them to enjoy themselves without commitment or legal consequences.

Abdul began to see how lucky he had been in life. He and his family had never had to endure such a dilemma or loss of face. The deprivations that had nearly destroyed him were of a different type. No one had ever violated his wife, and he was sure she would never be. Neither had any female member of his household as far as he knew.

He threw all his energy into his pupils and in helping them. Slowly, he began to heal and even started to inquire into the family he had left behind. The head administrator, who had been so kind to him from the beginning, was a man who had the interest of his nation at heart and tried to assist his fellows caught up in misfortune not of their making as best he could.

He would allow Abdul to use his mobile once every week, but his calls and texts remained unanswered. He wrote letters, sending them to all the addresses he once knew. Months went by, years, and he never received a single reply.

Then one morning, after sharing cloudy tea brewed from muddy water with his teaching fraternity, Mukteer, the Mercury of the camp, flew in with a mangled letter clutched in his dirty hands.

Abdul would be late for his lessons, but his mind had lost all place and time, and his heart was stuck squarely in his throat, trying its best to beat.

He stared at the letter long after its deliverer and his new friends had departed. Then, taking a deep, shuddering breath, he tore it open carefully. On the plain wrinkled sheet was the undisciplined and broken scrawl of an uneducated hand.

Dear Mr Abdul, my old friend.
As-salaam 'Alaykum.
Great joy overcame me when I saw your letter. Allah is great.
Your faithful wife and family have journeyed to America. Seek them there if you can.
They are well and long for you.
Your words took a long and winding path to my front door, and many eyes would have seen it on its flight to help steer it into my hands.
My son in law — you remember me talking of him - the chatterbox bus driver?
Fortunately, he has friends in every corner. Through them, I hope this letter finds you well.
Malik.

Abdul was overjoyed. His world seemed almost normal again with this one connection to the past. He re-experienced the breeze on his skin as he opened his shop doors for morning business carrying with it the warmth and sweet fragrance of Jasmine. After all, life was good, and he rushed to the admin offices with a smile on his face. He had not forgotten his students, but another hour of waiting would not improve their attentiveness anyway, so there was nothing there to lose.

He found the kind man interviewing yet another expectant entrant. The line seemed to be growing from one day to the next - not a good sign for his divided and exhausted country. Not wanting to put off his news for a later hour, Abdul sat on the wooden bench under the shaded overhang outside and waited, his thoughts racing.

A soft voice called him back from his daydreaming.

'Is there something I can do for you, Abdul?'

Finding himself unable to speak, Abdul thrust the opened letter at his friend and adviser. The man took it, similarly wordless, and read it, his face expressionless.

'This is long-awaited good news, Abdul. We now know that your family is safe and where they have gone. America is a big country, though. I will try my best to get further information. However, taking into account your circumstances, your friend Malik is trying to warn you. Someone is intercepting his mail, and because of this, they now know where you are. Time is not on your side. They will soon reach out to us, and we will not be able to refuse them. For your safety, you will have to move on.'

Abdul felt the familiar dreaded rot of despair creeping its way back into his heart. Some unknown entity, celestial or otherwise, was taking great amusement by tormenting him, teasing him into unexpected highs, and then dragging him down into unbearable lows. It was coming to that point when good occurrences were just as terrible as bad experiences – there was a growing and equal hate in his mind of them both.

'What do you mean?' he asked, but the answer was already plain to him.

'As a deflection for the callous disregard of our suffering, many rich nations sponsor promising and talented refugees. The numbers are insignificant, but it lets them use inflated words to hide the sparsity of action. You stand well placed for us to put you forward on this scheme, Abdul. You have connections. You have an education. You have experienced the worst and the best our country has to offer. The Americans will love your resume. For good or bad, it contains all the elements they love to espouse. The faster we can get you out of here, the better it will be for all.'

Abdul wandered away in a daze, not knowing what to make of what the head administrator had just told him. Had he complimented him or slotted him into a pigeon-hold as a lucky, privileged sod who eventually received more than his allotment, robbing those more deserving of the help available? In the end, Abdul didn't care. Finding Jasmine was the most crucial cause he had to live for, and he would sacrifice anything and anyone for it. Ideals were for those who could afford it. If sponsorship were his ticket out of this camp of sorrow, he would take it in the blink of an eye free of regret for those left behind.

Before another two months had gone by, Abdul found himself chauffeured out of the camp gates he had staggered through in what seemed a lifetime ago. It was hard for him to admit, but he had expected a fonder farewell from those he had become close during his stay. His pupils had hardly seemed to register what he was saying and continued in their everyday routine without pause when he had told them he was leaving. One teacher was the same as another for them. Their existence depended on what and who stood confined to the camp. Whatever or whoever went outside the fence no longer dwelled on this earth. The same rang true, it seemed, for his fraternity of teachers. They received his news with polite, knowing smiles, patted him on his back, and told him not to forget them. And that was that.

The administrator stayed a kind man to the very end. He had laboured hard to get all the relevant documents and had completed them in record time with a diligent and accurate hand. He drove Abdul personally to the airport and remained there until he had boarded his flight. His presence kept Abdul calm and reassured in the tenuous belief that all was well in this capricious world.

There was nothing wise or unique in his parting words, merely simplicity. Nothing asked or wanted in return.

'Your wife and life await you, Abdul. Find them and pursue meaning. Make the best of life's gifts.'

Abdul looked into his eyes, shook his soft hands, and turned his back. So preoccupied was he that to his eternal shame, he neglected to say thank you and goodbye - three words that would have gone a long way, maybe not so much for the administrator, but certainly for Abdul – an anchor to make him a better person than he was.

CHAPTER XIV

Anxious, uprooted, belonging neither to the outward consumerism of American culture nor the Afghani one left behind for various reasons formed a dichotomy of disparate impressions that shadowed Jasmine's new world.

Here in Fremont's "Little Kabul", she attempted to rediscover normality and her lost husband. In the mixing pot of displaced peoples and cultures, she focussed on providing a stable platform equipped with ever-changing coping strategies for her son.

No matter how much her father's previous status and his family's high level of education, they were still refugees and viewed with suspicion by the parochial outlook of the local authorities. They, her neighbours, had eighty per cent of their thoughts and concerns anchored in the war-torn land they had left behind physically, if not mentally. Their memories held an edited version of a non-existent idyll, but this rosy recollection served as comfort for them in this chosen place of exile. No matter how much they tried, there were always constant reminders, subtle and otherwise, that they did not belong. That feeling of displacement followed them like a fog everywhere, and the only reality they had to ground them was the fragmented one nearly obscured in their past. So they sought courage from those of similar and familiar backgrounds and recollections. In this new country where the paranoia of terrorism lay hiding under every rock, the burden of suspicion and condemnation was not a healthy one to carry. It was even worse for those born in this foreign place, for they did not even have their assured past to hold them steady and keep them bolstered against the waves of constant obstacles to acceptance. Integration was not an ideal to be acquired at any costs, especially that of self and culture. The essences that made them who they were could not be merely put aside for the sake of expediency.

Due to Dr Mamuud Mohammad's connections, life in Little Kabul was comfortable. They had a modest one up, one down house in a walled garden situated on the tree-lined streets of a leafy suburb lying under the sheltered hillsides of Fremont. His near-perfect English and impeccable qualifications allowed him to run a small medical practice catering mainly to the resident Afghans of Little Kabul. How he managed to pull that one off was anybody's guess. Already Jasmine could see her clever father cultivating his little garden to grow a future enterprise similar to the one circumstances had forced him to abandon. She admired him on the one hand and resented him on the other.

'Abdul is no longer with us, Jasmine,' he said to her one morning before leaving for work. 'Accept it. You have his son. Put your energies into giving him a life here that he could have only dreamt of back home. Make Abdul proud.'

His words were unsympathetic and devoid of empathy. The practical foundation he had based his life's actions and success on was now naked and laid bare for all to see. Had he become this way because of the rebellious behaviours of her little brother? Now a teenager, he had joined the local youth gangs of Freemont and was hardly ever at home. A father is always most hurt by rejection from their sons. To them, it's the mark of failure, an unremovable spot on their character and competence.

The private or, as the local Americans put it, the insular attitude of her new Afghan community would ensure that her ambitious father would rise only so far. If he tried too much, they would rapidly label him as a sellout, an *Amreecayee*. If this happened, he would lose his growing reputation, his clients and the prestige he sought. The world he strived to dominate and control was shrinking in around him.

Jasmine didn't care about any of that. She wanted her son to attend a good school, make friends, and excel in something practical at the end of it. Most of all, she wanted her husband back, to have him by her side as they watch their son grow into manhood in this strange land. He was somewhere in the old country. Maybe he had lost his way, languishing, possibly hurt, Allah forbids, but somehow she knew he was alive. She refused to accept any other alternative. Abdul was naïve and unprepared for this world and humanity's delusional constructs, but he was a fighter on a level hard for a casual observer to detect. You had to be very close to him to see this determination, and if Abdul had anything to fight for, it was for the love he had for her. If all existence was just our minds' hallucination, then this last was the one worth having.

Every week she sent out batches of emails and letters, to her cousin in Lashkar Gah, to Abdul's mother and aunt, to old friends and contacts, to embassies, both in Afghanistan and Pakistan, even to those in Iran and India. She even reached out to refugee camps. Only Malik bothered to reply, and his words contained only regret.

Jasmine's nights surrounded her with ghosts and phantoms who circled continuously, calling pitifully. She tried to go to them, terror and frustration weighing down on her heart, her feet mired in wet clay as thick, rolling fog obscured their faces and contorted their voices. She could even feel the dampness on her skin. Sometimes she sensed that Abdul was among these restless wraiths, but others were far from benign and friendly. They held her husband in their thrall and taunted her, daring her to free him if she could. Alas, the more she tried, the more she felt helpless and powerless. Mornings found her tired, sweaty and heavy with despondency. The only joy that kept her going was her healthy but quietly observing baby son, her little Abdul.

Leaving Little Kabul, even for short forays, was always a stressful and challenging undertaking. It was the same, she imagined, for a fish trying to cross dry land to get to another pond. Everything that she had achieved and accomplished back home in Afghanistan that raised her as one of the privileged was, if not negated, reduced to something insignificant in the eyes of these people who believed wholeheartedly in the exceptionalism of America. She stood exposed as a pretender, as someone not worthy. Her accent denounced her proficient command of the English language, her lack of knowledge of local colloquialisms left her stranded. Her mode of dress, which marked her as a respectable woman of Islam, left her open to ridicule and cheap humour. Even those who thought themselves kind spoke to her as if she were an idiot or, at best, a child. To react with indignation to these base assumptions only made things worse and to bear them with a rounded shoulder only confirmed the ignorant in their righteousness. Yet, at the same time, the inward-looking community that sheltered her limited and chained her to their past ways. Women should be dutiful, obey, and, most of all, remain silent. Once a bastion of support, her mother, now lost and fearful of her very own shadow, had become the worse of these spiritual prison wardens. Everything Jasmine did or attempted to do became shadowed by breathless, hyperventilated warnings.

Rather than give in to these lines of containment, Jasmine began to lead a double life. On the surface, she adapted a demure persona, seemingly complying with the restrictions and perceptions of others who thought they knew best. She learnt to drive and bought a small second-hand car with the last of her savings under the pretence that she had no one else to take her son around for the essentials, school, health checks, play, you name it - all the things needed to grow a healthy child in western society. It was frowned upon but passed the litmus test if barely.

Secretly, she adopted a pen name and began reaching out to other Afghan enclaves in the US, mainly in New York. Her pen became her sword of independence, or rather, her computer's keyboard did and her domain the world. She wrote dozens of articles and dispatched them to every ethnic and liberal publication she could find. At first, all she received back in return were refusals and rejections. She remained adamant, and nothing would deter her, doggedly sticking to writing, refining her pieces to focus on refugees and particularly the experiences of women refugees. One by one, her articles were accepted, and she was shocked then nearly overwhelmed by the response letters her growing readers began sending her, almost all using the cloak of anonymity. She had found her voice.

At the start, her stories covered versions of her experiences - her loss of home, culture and her husband's disappearance. A deliberate ruse perhaps to connect with someone who might have encountered Abdul on the long road from Kabul. However, as the soul-wrenching letters she received highlighted the plights of countless uprooted people, her articles began to take on a deeper meaning that reached the consciousness and hearts of sufferers and observers alike. Through her skilful pen, they, too, had found a voice.

At the core of all this was her yearning for Abdul. He was not merely her love, her child's father, but her life. She poured all of her heartbreak and loneliness into her stories, causing a cathartic release through the tears of her addicted readers wherever they were in the world, especially in America.

People began to wonder who this author was, not just in the name of curiosity but a desire to join with a soulmate, someone who understood the pain inside that remained unspoken and imprisoned by circumstance and culture.

The search was on. However, not even Jasmine's publishers knew who she was or whether she was male or female. All they were interested in was that her readership was growing at an exponential rate. She was good for business. Payment lay transacted through the volatile currency and anonymity of Bitcoin. They didn't even know her whereabouts or her true nationality. She was an angel of light sending her rays into the hidden darkness of her readers' lives and coins into their company's coffers. Her allure was irresistible and grew with each passing day. She was a mystery that had to be solved which naturally, increased her value to them.

No one in her family was aware of or suspected her actual occupation or the far-reaching success it had brought her. They thought her depressed and unable to cope with her new life as she spent so much time behind closed doors in her little upstairs bedroom. They worried for her health but did not approach her as they had no idea how to help and did not want to bring shame to the household by inviting in the services of outsiders—especially these foreign Americans with their brash, public ways. The family would cope with the problem, which meant, of course, that they would never do anything.

Thankfully, mental or otherwise illness was not one of Jasmine's burdens, although she had many. She kept her newfound wealth and fame secret and only spent her earnings modestly, mostly on things for her growing son. She found that she needed very little for herself but paid out a fair portion of her income hiring so-called professionals, reputable and not so much, to track down Abdul's location or at least discover what had become of him.

The trail tentatively started when he exited that bus at Jalalabad's station and lay mostly cold from that point of disappearance. Malik was indispensable as her man on the ground with these clandestine enterprises, although she made sure to compensate him handsomely for his efforts. He was a person to trust, but it didn't hurt to oil his hands in the process. It turned out that Malik had many unusual connections for an honest man and had many a finger in unexpected pies. He never once questioned the source of her wealth, although he might have privately examined it. This concern was one of her least. She had an objective, and while she had the means, nothing would stand in her way.

However, there was some news due to Jasmine's investments. Whether this was encouraging or disheartening depended on her mood when she woke in the morning. As described by the Afghan security forces, they had arrested a villain of a truck driver. His suspicious activities on the highway between Jalalabad and Lashkar Gah were flagged up and brought to their notice. Passengers, known to have disappeared mysteriously en route after bribing a lift on his distinctively decorated lorry was not an encouraging sign. After several vociferous complaints and accusations from concerned and upset relatives, they pulled the culprit over for questioning. As a result of using particular and unmentionable persuasive techniques designed to make him talk, he eventually sang a song of revelation. One of his tales seems to match a young man's fate who resembled Abdul in the description as he was already on the security agents' radar. Although of low priority, it alerted their attention. Abdul, regrettably, they said, had been handed over by this disreputable criminal into the hands of insurgent bandits like many other young men before and after him. The best they could do was list him as among the missing.

At least, this unsettling information confirmed that her husband was still alive at that point, if obviously, not well and in a safe condition.

Then the most recent news from Malik arrived in the form of a much wrinkled and creased letter that had no original date mark on it. Some American stamps were plastered unevenly on it, and she assumed someone had brought it into America and posted it from somewhere in New Jersey.

She tore it open with shaking fingers and read Malik's spider's hand, written as ever in broken Arabic. In this day and age, you would think that the man would have a computer or a mobile. Regardless of the beliefs of those misinformed, Afghanistan was not a country locked in the middle ages, but certainly, Malik was. The date at the top was from four month's past.

Her mother found Jasmine sitting there staring out of her window when she did not respond to her calls for lunch. It did not occur to ask what was troubling her daughter, for they were all a little afraid of her strange behaviour of late. Jasmine was happy with that. The more they left her alone, the better.

Malik had received a letter from Abdul. All this time, he had sat languishing in a refugee camp in Pakistan. Now with a bit of luck, he knew that she was now in America.

Her heart was pounding in her chest, and she wasn't sure if she should laugh or cry. Her husband was getting closer to her embrace, kisses and the joy of his son.

CHAPTER XV

Fame brought many unexpected difficulties. Any semblance of privacy was the first to fly out of the window. For Caterina, this felt as if someone had reached inside her and torn her clothes off, exposing not only her body in nakedness but her most intimate thoughts as well, eviscerated. She wanted to run but knew she would never find a place to hide, and if she did, she would always regret leaving behind what she had now found with the Afghan.

Something in the Afghan was changing. When they danced, they were joining in a way they had never done before. It was as if he were dressing her in a personal memory he could never share. He was fusing whatever person that animated that intimate dream with her, draping her in the same clothes, recreating Caterina into the form of this phantasma. She wasn't sure how she felt about that. Still, it brought them closer together, not only physically but spiritually, allowing their artistic skills to burgeon and ascend into areas none of them had ever explored. To watch them perform was an out of body otherworldly experience.

Yet, beneath it all, she felt that something was failing inside her. After every performance, where she once experienced elation and euphoria, she now sensed a growing hole of tiredness and weariness that was all-encompassing. Where she once desired nothing more than to make passionate love to her partner in creativity, she now only wanted to hold him gently to her breasts and drift happily off into blessed sleep. He never objected or resisted but flooded her with an empathy that came from somewhere deep within his complicated psyche. She knew that he realized that all was not well with her and wanted to help in the little way she needed.

She was terrified to discover what was ailing her, but as her health deteriorated in sync with their punishing if rewarding schedule, she had no recourse but to see her doctor. The news was as bleak as she had secretly dreaded.

They had been on a roller-coaster of a ride that had taken them to ever-ascending heights. The audience's ecstatic reception had blown Caterina away like a person standing at the edge of a cliff during a roaring tempest, the sea's waves pounding on the rocks below and the wind tearing through her hair. Never had she experienced such a rush of joy and euphoria. They had trashed all competition on their first outing on TV. Their photos appeared overnight in magazines and local papers. They were a raging topic on social media, with many Influencers waxing lyrical about their performances and interpretations. They were on the up and up, but for her, the time remaining was short - the Father's way of reminding us that we were human after all - made in his image but not a god despite our pretensions.

The tempo of their dances altered, instigated by the genius that was the Afghan. She would become rapidly breathless with the faster pieces, unable to hold to the pace. He sensed these changes and what others thought were merely signs of happiness, he instinctively knew that something was wrong on a deeper level and severe. His concern wasn't for the ending of a career before it had adequately even started. In reality, he didn't care one jot for such things. His worry was empathic, a genuine connection that science could not explain, the greatest gift of humanity, a human touch one for the other without any thought of gain. She felt this and loved him even more for it. She realized now that it was who the Afghan indelibly was, an innocent with a shy soul blessed with maturity – more so than most people would ever attain. Their dances became more personal, intricate and without doubt, spiritual. During their performance, the audience remained hushed, entranced, their eyes devouring every step, every turn, sinuous and graceful. They were not two separate dancers, but one, joined by an aura of exquisite expertise and sensuality. The music and the dance was everything.

Elena was blind and impervious to the personal battle that Caterina was undergoing. All she saw was the success of each performance and the mystic multi-coloured rainbow arching ahead, leading to that so far elusive pot of shimmering gold. Elena was ever racing before them, working night and day with frenetic energy to pave the road to ever more venues and shows. She did not have time to muddle cuddle her performers only to chivy them to more extraordinary exertions and higher attainments.

Then, one night during a routine of perfection, the first fatal misstep occurred, the one already written in Caterina's fate and that she had been expecting as she would a poisonous snake hidden in the grass. It was only a matter of time. The error was so sleight that only she and the ever-attentive Afghan detected it. A tenuous misalignment, a tiny cough and a spot of blood at the corner of her painted lips. Her world had changed.

'You have cancer, Caterina. We will have to refer you to a specialist right away for treatment, I'm afraid.'

Her doctor had tried his best to express sorrow and empathy. His many years of training and impersonal practice had reduced him to an automaton who saw systems rather than people. Blaming the man was a tad unfair—

tools of the trade and all that.

'It's in your lungs, Caterina. You've waited far too long before coming to us. It may have spread. We have no time to waste.'

Her fault again, it seemed—no reluctance on his part to lay blame then. Always herself to be culpable. Not the hyper-expensive medical insurance that she had only recently been able to afford.

Yes, she did smoke. Not as much as before, but it kept her weight down and calmed her nerves. A dancer needed these little tricks, the alluring wisps of white smoke, red lipstick, music and cocktails. Unless, of course, you were the Afghan. He required very little of anything. This weakness or perhaps strength was evident from the beginning. He was a man, born with magic.

She kept her sad news to herself. The only person she felt a tug to share it with was the Afghan. But he already knew all was not well with her and was giving her all he could. Would he miss her when she was gone?

As for Elena. Well, yes, she would be shocked. But it was a shame to admit that the cogs in her head would race around the knotted problem of replacing Caterina so the milk float could continue on its rounds. The show must go on, after all. She had her friend's measure - always had.

Her mother and sister? They would cry the tears of loss - burying her before she was dead. 'How could you be so selfish, Caterina?' Yes, yes, sorry, I have cancer. I didn't mean to inconvenience your life. Have you chosen your clothes for the funeral yet?

She couldn't think of anyone else who was still there to play a role in her life and upcoming death—this sober realization despite the many who had entered and exited her revolving doors. Living, in the end, was simply a waste of time.

Still, she kept her chin up, her smile fixed, and danced with the Afghan beyond the point of perfection. Her illness, her exquisite finesse and inventiveness seem to advance hand in hand, step to step. Their dance routines grew surreal, a mystical world of love and tragic mythology. The tempo slowed to a soulful throb. Their thighs entwined, sinuous, abdomens sliding erotically across each other, stirring the loins of the participants as well as the spell-bound on-lookers, a drumbeat of hearts thumping on ribcages, the gasping of breaths. Everything was lost and gained in the moment, lovers caught in the most intimate act, held fast in passion, submerged inside each other, pushed onwards by the shadowed voyeurs glimpsed at vision's periphery. Her weakness at the end added to the semblance of orgasmic glow, a surrendering to her partner, physically and emotionally, leaning in on him in complete trust, arms draped over his shoulders, parted lips, touching his, her eyes sultry and lidded. The illusion was so thorough that it had become a reality.

Elena was angry. This undesired news was a slap in the face, an outrageous intrusion. The hags that pulled the mythical strings were prancing with glee in her path once again. Like bored immortals, they were toying with her destiny, taunting her. Life was a bitch, but she knew well how to deal with its ilk. They were so close, and now this. Caterina was like a child. She should have taken better care of herself, and such a thing would not have happened. In her opinion, Caterina had always been selfish, interested in the narcotics of life – sex, cigarettes, wild music, and alcohol. Maybe Caterina should have paid more attention to her art and the profits it could generate rather than her cheap desires and what lay between her legs. Was she cruel? Perhaps, but she was furious. It was just like Caterina to find some way to cop out when the going was really good. Yes, yes, she would stay by her side through all the treatment and hospitals, but in the meantime, Elena would have to find someone as Caterina's understudy. The fly in the ointment here was whether or not that weird Afghan fellow would dance with anybody else. Who could tell what went on in that mind of his? And, if the lights were even on in there. He was more like a bloody zombie than a living, breathing, human being.

When Caterina had first revealed her news, Elena had felt a shiver of cold air at the nape of her neck, the Grim Reaper's breath, and the tiny hairs there rose in response. She had experienced numbness and an unusual displacement of her senses. In the rarified atmosphere of suspended concentration, she had stopped listening to the voice telling her of things she preferred not to hear. Her instinct was to cover her ears and scream – 'Shut up, shut up. Go away,' – over and over again. Instead, she had found herself nodding, cooing, and holding Caterina in her arms, whispering how they would get over it together, find a solution, 'Things are never as bad as they seem, my dearest.'

Was she a hypocrite? Yes, she was, and a coward as well. She should have told Caterina there and then that what goes around comes around. That her self-centred, indulgent ways and come back to bite her on her dancer's firm, rounded backside. With that thought, she had experienced sudden and inappropriate arousal blown in on the sprite winds of nostalgic memory. She once lingered kisses on that particular part of Caterina's anatomy.

Give Caterina her due. She never faltered in her performances. Instead, she and the Afghan had elevated them to the heights of the very heavens. They were the dancing saints, although there was nothing religious in their routines – quite the opposite. Their collaborations were becoming sensualized to the point of a surreal sexual experience, leaving the audiences exhausted at the end, sensations long-dormant and buried, teased into the open and set alight. Caterina's approaching date with mortality had awakened all the emotion and talent held within – her creative gates, thrown wide open. Their fame was spreading like a forest fire, and the coffers were brimming over with appreciative revenue. It was a delectable, bitter-sweet moment for Elena, one that she both savoured and dreaded.

Abdul did not want to lose that wispy, tenuous link that connected him to this troubled woman who breathed psychic life into his dying spirit and anchored him to the memory of the only reason he had to live. He felt something inside her fading away and opened up himself to merge with her, wrapping the music and the dance around her slim form. They were so close that with every step, each turn and pirouette, Abdul felt the fluttering of her heart as it strived to join the beat and rhythm that was more than music but was life itself. He sensed that on the day she stopped dancing, would come that hour when she would lie down and die. This outcome was the last thing he wanted to happen, so he fused with her in intimacy and the harmony of movement. They did not dance for others, merely for themselves, keeping each other from passing through that ethereal, gently blowing curtain that called to them constantly. They had linked in life to prevent each other from crossing into death's shadow. It was not an endeavour they could keep up forever, but the fear of the outcome when the music finally hushed kept them going – silence was that black spot. As the flesh on her bones began to thin, so did his. Yet the poignancy of their performances only increased. To watch them was like listening to counter-point in Mozart's music, ever spiralling beyond the senses, untouchable and unpredictable, enjoying the drifting, lofty heights, yet filled with trepidation of the inevitable fall when it stopped.

Eventually, as they all knew that it would, the wheel ceased to turn, grinding to a halt under the frailties of human flesh. Even indomitable will could not overcome that mark etched in nature's sand. Caterina danced till she could no longer stand, her once beautiful and expressive eyes ringed and dull from the sickness gnawing on her insides, her vibrant body now a virtual collection of bones. In the small apartment where she had spent most of her adult years, she passed over the threshold of life, gazing into the eyes of the man who had put meaning back into her existence. At the final moment, she smiled, her grip tightening on the hand that held hers.

Elena, who was present as she had promised, witnessed it all. She could not see the Afghan's visage beneath the shroud of his hair, but by Caterina's reaction, her friend could only have seen what she always longed to see in his enigmatic face. For the first time in her life that she could remember, the tears flowed freely and unchecked down Elena's cheeks.

CHAPTER XVI

America lacked the true meaning behind family and culture. It was a violent place that not only built an industry around war but glorified it. Its people lay sold on the myth of the Wild West and frontier town where strong men were loners and carried guns on their hips. This concept, to them, was the ultimate expression of freedom, independence, justice and patriotism. Ownership meant everything to them, and they saw themselves as lords of the world sanctified by God who lived in corporate America. Abdul thought that he had left war and violence behind, but in this land of self-illusion and the absence of organized warfare since the time of Abraham Lincoln, he cringed in fear from the raw conflict written on the face of every man and woman he examined. Even that act of enquiry held a great danger. Most perceived it not as an attempt to understand but as a challenge. By an outsider, and an infidel at that. So he soon learnt to keep his gaze down. The ignorant and the bigot seemed always lying in wait for an excuse to swagger. They would reach for that metaphorical holstered pistol at every perceived insult – ever the oversensitive believers in their exceptionalism. The right to bear arms and defend one's liberty, whatever that was, remained alive and well in the psyche of these guilt burdened people. The fertile lands on which they built the delusion of hope and glory was not theirs in the first place. So they adhered to the maxim that might make right - and so began a new phase of life in these here United States of America for Abdul.

It was not an auspicious beginning, and Abdul was constantly faltering one step before the fall into homelessness. He did not have family, a sponsor, nor a patron. In America, to receive benefits was a sign of poverty, and to be impoverished was not merely a failure. It was a sin. Even the state's servants who doled out the means to stay alive were believers in the false dream. They expected you to come to them on hands and knees, and if you did not, they ensured that you suffered even more. Their eyes did not look upon you, for it would be to acknowledge your existence if they did so. You were the American bogeyman, the example of what happened to those not strong enough to benefit before the altar of the capitalist cathedral and the law of Darwin, the survival of the fittest. They could not admit to themselves, or perhaps did not see, that they were acolytes to eugenics, inheritors of the Nazi ideal.

The bureaucracy of day to day survival was relentless. The system from food stamps, refugee support, rental cheques, on and on, was so complicated and time-consuming that Abdul did not have a spare moment for anything else. His rudimentary command of English made these impossible tasks even more difficult. He became accustomed to being sneered at, treated as dumb and uneducated, dismissed and ignored. He had become a persona non grata, vermin, worthless and a nuisance. Refusing to lie down and die, he persevered, holding fast to a green-eyed smile and the tendrils of a plucky Spanish song. He carried these memories with him everywhere he went, not anticipating, not hoping, just moving from sunrise to sunset, one effort flowing into the next.

In Afghanistan, decades of war were so long-lasting that children grew into adulthood not knowing anything else, and fighting and killing were the norm. Still, there was family, identity and tribal belonging. Strangely, this eternal grinding of invasions and social destabilization incongruously grew men of pure gold. They were lords of dignity and good thinking, but on the other hand, some men were jackals through and through, bereft of any deserving quality to mark their humanity. The label animal usually lay reserved for these dregs, but this was a gross misnomer for nothing in the animal kingdom would conduct itself in such a way except the beasts belonging to the human race. Abdul encountered a few of the former in this land of supposed refuge, and they refreshed his dwindling spirit. However, he mainly met the latter, dressed up as civilized citizens. They carried with them a cloying miasma akin to clinging, melted tar, sucking at whatever light Abdul had regained. What would he have found if this land of red, white and blue had been invaded time and time again by foreign nations seeking dominium and international influence? If this country of laws and justice lay so overrun with wolves, what would he have found then?

New York, the gateway to equal opportunity, was a savage place. He did not understand the legal rules or the unwritten ones. Nor could Abdul make good sense of them even when he understood their history and purpose. He did what any sane man with nothing to lose would do. He ran away.

For Abdul, crossing America's hinterland from East to West was a study of loneliness and isolation. Everything was new and carried the tinge of suspicion and hostility, even down to the rocks and vegetation. He was so filled with hesitancy and defensiveness that to marvel at anything was to tempt the fear of some unexpected reprisal for offences his very presence provoked. He turned ever and ever inward to inure himself against rejection and hardship, begging at the corners of cities and small towns he encountered to put food into his wasting body. Now and again, he met men and women who stood made of better stuff than their fellows. Some gave him odd jobs to do, feeding and sheltering him from the ravages of the elements and the scorns of others less able to see beyond their vulnerabilities. Others offered him lifts along the long asphalt road, designed for the automobile, which the petrochemical companies had so successfully implanted within the American dream, transporting him a little further along the endless route. To walk in this country of the Anglo Saxon God was an anathema.

His second-hand designer sneakers, presented as a welcome package when he first entered the United States, were now worn and threadbare, their soles as thin as his grasp on reality and with his toes poking out the top, exposed and bleeding. Somewhere along the line, a craggy old woman with blue piercing eyes and a no-nonsense voice gave him another pair which she said once belonged to her husband. The good for nothing, she said, was seven feet under and had no further use for them. They were a size too big, but he was more than grateful, keeping them slung over his shoulders for as long as he could to preserve them and a kind memory.

Abdul spoke less and less and soon forgot that he had a voice. The people he ran into, good or bad, were more interested in hearing themselves, and it didn't matter whether he spoke or not, as all they ever wanted to do was talk. Very few knew how to listen. Abdul learned how to listen for all of them. It fed his thoughts and the conversations that never left his head.

The state police patrols became his biggest deliverers. In their disdain and hostility, they would pluck him from the empty stretches of the scorching, sometimes freezing roads and dump him into a nice cell where he slept like a felled log – blessed moments of reprieve. Soon they realised that they had no idea what to do with this immigrant vagrant or did not want to take the time to find out and would eject him back into the world with threats to move on, or else. Abdul did not care, and one day was as good as the next.

He seemed to have merged with the landscape, and cars would roar by night and day, with its occupants completed unaware of his existence. He lived in a stratum that they did not wish to see. He was invisible for most and a brute to be beaten into submission to assuage inherited guilt by others.

These predators, mainly mal-educated, underachieving, young, white males, but not always so, were the greatest danger to his physical wellbeing. It suited Abdul well on his journey through hostile Indian Territory to borrow the term from the white supremacist handbook to remain below the inhabitants' radar. This aim was not always successful. Sometimes when he thought himself alone in blessed isolation, the wind his only companion, a vehicle, driven by ill-will and restless malcontents would fly upon his rear. Their unprovoked assault would force him to dive headlong into the dirt-covered layby to preserve his life and limb, a victim to rage he had no willing part in engineering.

Abdul endured through the beatings, the kicking and the raucous jeering and name-calling. He grew immune to it all. And when they became bored and tired of punishing the unprotesting, they would race away even the heavier with guilt's burden, not a whimper uttered by their victim despite their desperate and brutal efforts to make someone, anyone, pay.

Abdul would pick himself up achingly out of the dust and carry on as if nothing had happened, embracing the silence and the emptiness. The bruises were livid and painful, but they belonged to someone else, a dull throbbing in the background somewhere. He was alone but not always lonely. What others referred to as the middle of nowhere was a haven of comfort to him. The pale blue sky was his roof, the dirt under his feet a carpet and the bushes his bed.

The people of this foreign land had become the lice he sought to avoid, but they were everywhere, biting and itching his skin and mind irritably at every opportunity. He didn't mind the long detours to avoid them, but the task was the same as tip-toeing through an ant's nest. So, yes, by default, his place of preference was solitude.

In the end, it was a lilting Spanish melody that kept pulling him westwards. It remained undefined, the echo of several tunes mixed into one, in the midst of which an ethereal face with mesmerizing green eyes danced in and out, beckoning him with her laughter of joy and innocence. He followed her onwards and inwards, hearing and seeing everything yet feeling nothing.

Abdul had the gift of stamina a long-distance runner would envy. However, the reason for his survival was down to the Maliks of this world. And, of course, the likes of that old farmer who hummed to him every time he lay down to sleep. A weary body longing to stop but, for some unknown reason, could not—the crunch of each footstep in the dirt his only timepiece on his never-ending journey. Now and again, this ticking metronome chimed, and a pure soul would intervene with a necessity that would revitalize Abdul to endure the next stretch of road, the next mountain, the next hostile city.

Small town America was not just a place in time but a state of mind. Most of the people that subsisted in these industrial and economically forgotten spaces lived captured in a time warp, their world frozen at a standstill. A people left behind by progress that no longer required them, a frontier's dream and vitality broken, a mad rush that had washed up against the cliff of expediency with nowhere else left to go. They walked their empty streets resentfully, angry and intolerant - severed from the false dream they saw as their right to partake in. They were left suspended, captured by the belief in conspiracies and adherence to a truculent anti-establishment stance. The elites and foreigners were out to get them, riding on the red steeds of communism and the white of libertarianism. They were the representation of the anti-Christ and had to be resisted if not defeated. The last stand of the Alamo was alive and well – it remained, as always, the call to arms. Abdul's bedraggled and dejected presence passing through their strongholds, uninvited and unwanted, was just another invasive sign that the old gates of patriotism lay broken and hanging on rust eaten hinges. They watched him come and go with impotent violence simmering in their squinted eyes.

Eventually, Abdul found himself washed up on a golden strip of sand where breaking surf, fretting and gurgling, barred his way. Like drifting flotsam without aim or purpose, he could go no further and sat down on the playground of the blind and privileged to contemplate the emptiness that lay before him. It was a beautiful glowing morning, too early for the self-centred and self-loving youth, both old and young, for this was the land of everlasting life, to rise tired from their nighttime epicures. He had intentionally stolen a small pocket of peace for himself, a token from Allah who, it seems, had not forgotten him.

Of course, the good-intentioned were always righteously defensive of what they felt by right was theirs to preserve against the malice of the disfranchised. From behind curtained windows, Abdul was soon identified as an anomaly and reported to the guardians of the unimaginative and unchanging status quo. What was good for them was right for them. The reincarnation of the sheriffs from the myth filled ages, plucked from the pages of an old Wild West novel, hands-on holsters and fingers twitching, they advanced on the lone figure lost in deep contemplation and communion, loud voices demanding identification and purpose. Abdul had none to show and was carted away in the modern version of a prison wagon, judged and sentenced before proven guilty. It is something that stood reinforced time and time again that he was not allowed to forget. In America, to be poor and homeless was a sin. In this God's land, the witnesses approved, fearful of their very own downfall, condoning the improper rites of justice and punishment. Remove the stain, and God bless America.

The police of the sunshine state harangued Abdul for what seemed like hours. They appeared to think that he was more than he was or, perhaps, they hadn't got anything else better to do. He didn't care. By now, he knew the drill by heart. Finally, fed up with this idiot of an immigrant, they locked him in a cell for the night. It was his lucky number, for he had one all to himself. He promptly fell asleep on the squeaky little cot.

'Wakey, wakey, my stinky immigrant bird! You've got a visitor.'

The loud voice accompanied by a clattering noise woke Abdul. He stayed where he was lying and tried to focus on the object of the disturbance.

'Stop that, Daniel. He is a person like you and me. There is no need to call him names.'

'Suit yourself, Shirley. Yell for me when you've had enough.'

The woman standing in front of the bars had long black hair and green eyes. Abdul was having difficulty breathing.

'Hi there,' she said brightly. 'I'm a volunteer social worker for this here beach county. Aren't we all so lucky! You can call me Shirley.'

Abdul couldn't care less what her name was. She had green eyes, and that was all he saw. Such a simple coincidence, yet to him, it meant everything.

'Didn't anyone tell you that it's rude to stare?'

Her effervescence and unfiltered directness brimmed over, catching Abdul's buried attention. He thought it childlike and endearing, and it drew him like a butterfly to a lone lamp in the middle of the mountains.

> Round and round
> On wings so light
> To find my way
> On this black night
> So beautiful the blaze
> That holds my gaze
> Round and round
> With all my strength
> I must fly higher
> Oh, how bright I am
> My wings' are on fire.

Why this poem from his childhood should resurface now, Abdul had no idea. Maybe it held a warning in it, a premonition reflected in the script, reaching over space and time to protect him. His mother always said that he was a useless dreamer. Perhaps there was more than a grain of truth in that.

'So, will you tell me your name? It's only fair, you know. I've given you mine.'

She was the all American girl he had seen in the movies – bubbly, external joy filling the spaces with smiles, exuberance and nothing is impossible attitude, all cotton candy, pink and fluffy. She was a page torn straight out of an Archie comic. And, those green eyes, sparkling like gems, hinting at sexuality that shone through with guile, perhaps, the woman she was, or maybe innocent, like a teenage girl, still unsure of her blossoming body and the things that it could do. For such a long time now, his interest had never been so intrigued. It felt like an awakening of sorts – something entirely different with a touch of Jasmine to sweeten it and give it a perfumed scent.

'Abdul,' he murmured, his tongue fumbling over the almost forgotten sounds.

'Oh, Abdul. What a nice name. And where are you from, Abdul?'

Questions. Questions. Abdul was tired of interrogations no matter who was doing it. A cloud of resignation settled over him, and he did not answer.

She didn't seem phased by his silence and pushed on without hardly drawing breath, a dappled stream dancing over rocks and pebbles in carefreeness, filled with movement and confidence, assured of her spot in the universe.

'Well, this old jailhouse is not the place for you, Abdul. We'll have to get you out of here – somewhere more suitable.'

She shouted just loud enough so that anyone listening would clearly hear, and Abdul felt the performance was not merely for his benefit.

'And I know just the spot. Wouldn't you like that, Abdul?'

She smiled at him, her teeth, white and even, peeping through her curving lips, an evangelical billboard to heaven and optimism.

'Just got to do the paperwork for these silly men, Abdul, and then we'll be on our way, so you take it easy, you hear. Leave this all to me.'

Then she was gone.

Abdul sat down and waited. The hours ticked by, and the sunshine lady with green eyes did not return. A uniformed officer, crisply ironed, brought in a meal on a tin tray and handed it to him gingerly through a square gap in the bars. He sniffed loudly and wrinkled his nose before departing without a word. His opinion was eloquent enough.

Abdul took a few mouthfuls before his stomach began to threaten him, balling up in knots, trying to expel the unaccustomed substance in it. He put the tray aside and lay back down, waiting fatalistically for the unpleasant sensations to pass.

Well, those discomforting feelings did recede, but Miss America, for all her promising and encouraging words, did not reappear. To say that Abdul experienced disappointment was not entirely true. He had lost the ability to feel such unhelpful emotions a very long time ago – a man can only work with what is actually in his hands, and good intentions, voiced or not, were only mists. He drifted off to sleep, making use of the comfort he knew would not last.

The following morning, Abdul woke disorientated. It took him many moments to remember where he was and how he had gotten there.

'It's about time, sleepyhead. Are you ready to go?'

She had been watching him sleep. He was sure of that. For how long, he had no idea - as to why, well, that was an even greater mystery. Inexplicably, he felt pleased by her attention, whatever her motives were. She had also kept her promise, a point that was as rare as golden coins on this journey from somewhere to nowhere—a quest to find a green-eyed smile on the wispy trail of a Spanish melody.

'Daniel! Are you coming to open this door or not?' the girl who named herself as Shirley yelled.

'Don't get your panties in a twist. I'm coming,' grumbled the taciturn guardian shuffling into view. 'Anxious to take your new boyfriend home, are you?'

It was apparent to the watching Abdul that they knew each other or were familiar with one another over a long period – their relationship so far undefined. Anyway, it was none of his business. American women were unfathomable and behaved in ways unacceptable in his country – it was something he could never get used to.

'My panties are not your concern, Daniel,' she replied cheerfully, but there was a definite trace of a bite in the response – a deeper undertone of meaning.

As soon as the gate swung open, Abdul walked quickly through, following his rescuer. Even in his severely malnourished state, he couldn't help but glance at her rear, scantily covered by a pair of white shorts that exposed more than it covered. His concept of acceptable propriety advised him that it was proper under Allah for her to be arrested and corrected. Her deportment was unseemly and an offence. He quickly averted his gaze and his mind for who was he, a cast out and beggar, to judge and appoint a woman's place in society. A man should deal with his insecurities first before imposing them on a woman's body in the name of his god. Abdul sadly felt that he was losing his faith and his way. He was afraid of what was left, of who he was becoming.

'We've got to get you cleaned up, Abdul – a nice shower, some new clothes, perhaps? I'm afraid what you're wearing is falling apart at the seams, and all we'll get back if we put them in the washing machine are rags.'

She seemed to like talking. Whether to reassure herself or Abdul, he wasn't sure. Whatever. He liked the sound of her voice.

She drove him on a roller coaster ride in a noisy Volkswagen beetle to an outdated building not far from the beachfront. She said they kept it running through crowdfunding, whatever that was, and they were dedicated to getting people like him back on their feet and absorbed into society. The neighbours, she said, were irritated by their presence, but who cared about them and their property prices, they could think as they liked. Through all this, he kept quiet and listened, enjoying the movement of her lips as she spoke, not fully understanding the culture wars behind her cheery words.

'It's a good thing I saw you when they brought you in,' she continued. 'You're fortunate, Abdul. No idea what those Neanderthals would have done. Here we are. Let's introduce you to the others and get you registered, shall we? Oh, don't look so worried. This place has a license from the county hall. We're all good and proper.'

Abdul had no idea what she was talking about or what difference it all made, but he felt safe with her. She had green eyes and a beautiful smile.

'Hi, Shirley. Picked up another stray, huh?'

A stout matronly lady with iron-grey hair pulled back severely into a bun greeted them from where she was standing behind a reception desk as Shirley whisked Abdul through the peeling green entrance doors of the building. She seemed a rock of calm among the frenetic to and fro of the people crisscrossing her. Her floral bohemian dress fitted into the colourful surroundings where everyone talked with and over everyone else. Abdul tried to pick up on a conversation or two but gave it up as an impossible task and concentrated wholly on the exchange between Shirley and the receptionist, who was now surveying him with eyes that pierced through her tiny, round spectacles and penetrated his skin.

'This is Abdul, Emma. Abdul, meet Emma. If there is anything you need, Emma is your girl.'

'You do know that our house is already full to bursting, don't you, Shirley? Where shall we stick poor Abdul here? By the look of him, he's been to hell and back.'

'You'll find a way, Emma darling. You always do.'

'Excuse me a moment while I fetch my magic wand then,' said the receptionist, her brow furrowed into a scowl as she thumbed through a battered registry book.

'What's your surname, Abdul?' she asked without looking up.

'Abdali,' he replied, gripping onto the edge of the high desk to stop himself from being torn adrift by the unfamiliar eddies and currents pulling at his awareness.

The elderly lady immediately looked up, stabbing him with her icy-blue gaze.

'Afghani?'

It was almost a demand.

He nodded.

'Our Emma has spent her years crawling all over the Middle East and thereabouts,' said Shirley, filling Abdul in. 'She speaks perfect Arabic and Farsi. You wouldn't think it by looking at her, would you?'

Emma tutted under her breath.

Taking the hint, Shirley grinned broadly and pulled away.

'Abdul, darling. I've got to make my rounds. I'll drop by later to see how you're getting on.'

With that, she sashayed away, her rounded buttocks swaying and rolling. Abdul stared after her, mesmerized.

Emma's no-nonsense throat clearing brought his attention back quickly, and he flushed blood red with guilt. 'Sign here, Abdul Abdali, and remember to behave yourself during your stay with us. This sun-shine land is America. Don't forget it.'

Abdul accepted the rebuke with lowered eyes and did what she asked. If she weren't a woman, she would make a fine Imam.

When he had finished, she spun the book away from him and studied his script.

'You have beautiful calligraphy, Abdul. University educated?'

He nodded.

She looked him in the eyes once again as if trying to find the truth residing in his soul.

'Follow me, Abdul Abdali. Let's get you settled in.'

CHAPTER XVII

There was no sight or sign of him. They continually scrutinized every port of entry diligently for their mysterious client rewarded their efforts handsomely, and lawyers did not come cheap in capitalist America.
'Give me your tired, your poor, your huddled masses yearning to breathe free. The wretched refuse of your teeming shore....'
The guardians of the Statue of Liberty's ever-tightening skirts took this sonnet by Emma Lazarus very seriously indeed, if perhaps not in the same spirit as she might have intended. They scrupulously documented every dewy-eyed refugee blinded by hope who squeezed in beneath her mighty feet. Every glance, a look of disapproval. Each question loaded to strip the petitioner of self-worth – superiority confirmed through privilege. As an official recently claimed, 'We meant those words for Europeans.' What did he mean by that exactly? Only the self-righteous would dare pervert the message of a poet.
They must have logged the name of Abdul Abdali from Kabul, Afghanistan, somewhere. For their parochial western ears, it already carried a sound with the taint of the unknown, frightening, a bogey man with concealed knife and bomb – a threat of some vague and undefined invasion to their values and way of life. Still, their client would persist until the letters lay prized from beneath the reluctant fingers of some anonymous immigration clerk.
Jasmine checked the reports of these agents for pay every night before going to bed. As usual, Abdul's movements were ghostlike. Whatever environment he travelled through absorbed him, and he would disappear in the belly of the beast. So far, by luck or design, he had not been consumed. Not yet. He was so close now that her heart fluttered, causing a strange sickening sensation in her chest.
Then finally, when she was least expecting it, the news she was anticipating came. A refugee carrying her husband's name had arrived by plane from Pakistan to New York. Could it be any other than her Abdul? There was no way to tell for sure, but she would keep her hunters on the trail. Loneliness had a way of making even the most loyal go astray - at the most basic level, wasn't she a woman after all? She had desperate need of a husband and her

111

son, a father. His absence from her life was growing a large hole in her soul. She should never have sent him away. Facing hardship and danger together was what a family should do, wasn't it?

Her hired hounds tracked him down to the less than adequate accommodations the authorities had assigned him. He was not there, long flown the coup as was his habit. She didn't blame him. Alone in this culturally hostile land bereft of family and connections was a nightmare she couldn't begin to imagine. She drove herself to despair and distraction by mentally walking in his shoes. She knew it was futile and unhelpful for her peace of mind and no aid to Abdul whatsoever but couldn't stop herself from doing so. She consoled herself with the thought that now he was in America, he would be easier to find. That, too, was wishful thinking. For all its bluster on human rights and respect for a civilized society, America was a place of the disappeared. A person could wander forever and not be recognized, anonymous and invisible.

Her father rarely came home now, and when he did, he did not stay long, just like her wayward brother. That suited her fine, for they were growing more and more estranged, and she did not want him poking his nose into her affairs. What he did when away remained a great mystery, but there were signs that he had found someone else to share his pillow. A man needed pliant women to conquer to feel his waning power no matter his professed religion.

Her mother seemed oblivious. She watched television all day, seated on the sofa opiated and hypnotised by the endless drivel broadcasted to the masses. At night she took prescribed tranquillizers to help her sleep – thinking and dreaming held a deep terror for her like drowning alone far out at sea. They rarely spoke to each other any longer, although they shared the same small space daily. What was that old saying? Oh, yes. Ships passing each other during the night or words to that effect.

Her family had morphed into something unrecognizable, disintegrating before her eyes. In Afghanistan, where corruption, war and uncertainty surrounded them from dawn to dawn, they had been far better off than in this country of milk and honey. There was a great irony in that.

The famous New York Times had reached out to her requesting that she authored a weekly article for them. She was still thinking about that proposal for her pieces were still selling like hotcakes, and she had started writing a book. Many publishers were pushing to represent her if only she would produce a manuscript. Afghanistan and its woes were becoming the topic of the season for many top politicians in Washington. Knowledgeable, popular and sensitive writers were few and difficult to find. She was in demand and could set her very own price. As far as she could tell, she was a very wealthy woman and had selected an agency to represent her. It was the only way to keep the wolves from her front door. It was the last remaining strategy to stop the hyenas from discovering her true identity.

The feeling of time running out, of being under siege, enveloped her every single passing day. She emerged from her room only when the activities and necessities of her son called to her. She even considered hiring an au pair, but that would definitely get the fingers pointing and wagging in her direction. Suspicion and unwarranted attention were the last things she wanted. Besides, joining in with little Abdul's innocence was a joy she would never surrender despite the urgency in finding her husband. Her father kept insisting that her failure to release the past and create new opportunities for the future would destroy her in the end. She knew what he meant by that. Find a new husband to care for her, for she was merely a woman.

'You're still young. Plenty of time to have more children.'

Sometimes, when at her lowest ebb, she felt that there was some truth in that. However, in the end, it merely confirmed the callousness that resided inside the man she once adored. She had education, a newly discovered skill that, thankfully, had monetary value, a home and an ambitious and influential father. Like it or not, these things insulated and protected her. What about those less fortunate fellow dispossessed who had no such luck to fall back on? It was these people of little hope, scarce resources, and those who sought to help and understand them, who were the bountiful contributors to her livelihood. At times she felt an oppressive shame as if she were a vampire sucking blood from those whose veins were already running thin.

Another three years flew by, and Abdul's footsteps had faded and grown cold. Still, her heart continued to beat determinedly within a void. It was the only path she knew how to continue to reach her objective, ignoring sage advice and opinions wrapped up in pretend wisdom. It is easy to comment when you are but a spectator. Even her publishers had gotten in on the act, seeking to guide her to their ways as all patriarchs took blind pride in doing. It didn't matter whether they were men or women. The organizations they laboured for were masculine edifices and constructs. By now, they had guessed that the enigmatic writer who was more than a recluse was female and hence required their firm guiding hands. Jasmine kept them at bay, deflecting all approaches not based on business and the writing enterprise. Gradually, they began to get the message and developed a respect for their lucrative, if invisible asset.

One early evening, out of the blue, her mother called to her as she was passing through the sitting room with little Abdul, back from his Karate and Judo classes with which he had fallen in love. Usually, her mother would partially interrupt her viewing to hug her grandchild, and that would be it. This time, however, was different.

'Jasmine, dearest,' she called, rare excitement shining in her eyes. 'Come, look at this! It's wonderful!'

'What is it, Mum?' asked Jasmine, making a polite show of being interested.

'It's a competition, dear. A dance-off. Mostly Spanish and Argentinian dances. You used to be passionate about that if I can remember correctly.'

'That was a long time ago. Seems like a different lifetime now.'

'Come along, dear. Don't be a bore. Look, little Abdul is enjoying it. You have to see the next couple. They are spectacular! They call them the Afghan and the Signorina. My money is on them to win. No one can touch them.'

'The Afghan?' responded Jasmine, already intrigued despite her initial disinterest. 'That's unusual.'

'It is, dear. And they are. Sit. They're up next,' replied her mother, patting the seat next to her and sliding over to give Jasmine room.

Jasmine felt the years falling away from her as the Spanish beat and tempo transported her back to happier times. She felt her husband's arm around her waist as they twirled and whirled to a timeless Iberian melody, high on the illicit and private pleasure they were indulging in. The couple on the TV was quite good, if not exceptional, and her feet began to tap and her fingers drumming out the rhythm. She smiled and hummed to the jaunty tune, experiencing carefree happiness that had long evaded her.

'Here it comes,' said her mother, leaning forward in anticipation. 'My favourites.'

Jasmine laughed out loud, a tinkling of pure sound, caught up in the unexpected joy of the moment. Little Abdul clapped his hands in time with the music.

'Olay!'

A jarring, sliding tune filled with guitars and mandolins emanated from the large, flat-screened TV, crashing over their senses.

'Olay!'

'Doesn't it sound a lot like our music?' asked her mother breathlessly.

'Yes,' replied Jasmine. 'The Moors.'

Her mother glanced back at her, but Jasmine wasn't sure if she understood the connection. It wasn't important. They were all happy together like they used to be in the old days.

Then as the music's tempo increased, a statuesque woman, red rose in her black hair, appeared.

She was all that one would expect from a superb, professional dancer. She strode magnificently onto the dancing arena, shoulders drawn back, chin lifted, proud, and almost arrogant. Her muscled legs, gliding and strutting at the same time – a woman who met the world head-on, always facing into the winds of fate, never shrinking, never batting an eyelid. She took but never gave unless she wanted to. The blood of everyone, male and female, could not help but be stirred hot by this goddess of independence—the music, lilting and cajoling, curled around her seductive frame and carried her on.

'Wow!' exclaimed her mother, clapping her open palms to her flushed cheeks. Jasmine couldn't have stated it better. She felt herself on the stage with this woman, like to like, spirit to spirit. For her, it was as if they were sisters of a sort – a recognition across space and time, although divided at birth. One, expressing what the other had always wanted to, locked in by culture, freed by a proud heritage - reflections in a rippling pond.

Reaching her central point, the captivating dancer raised her long arms like swans' necks, fiery pink flamingoes even. Frozen, waiting, she challenged the audience with black kohl eyes and sensual red-painted lips – brimming with sexuality that no man would dare approach for fear of emasculation.

But, then, striding into frame came such a man. He was slender but exuded athleticism. Emerging like a warrior bent on confrontation, his progress towards his petrified target was deceptively fast even though every step seemed paced and calculated, his focus, rapier-sharp, unbreakable. A drama in the making.

His costume wrapped him, skin-tight as if painted onto his flesh, red with splashes of yellow, and beneath it, his body moved with sinuous grace. Despite her upbringing, Jasmine felt a heat rising in her response to this figure and his intent. He portrayed a man in masterful control of his world in which he knew how to dominate what he desired – male sexuality poured from his veins, and Jasmine felt herself drowning in it. He wanted that woman he was moving towards, and this predator intended to possess her now, in any way that he could. She had ceased to be merely a spectator, and something unexplainable had dragged her psyche into the screen, exciting it, stimulating it. Was there something familiar about that magnificent figure?

She was not the only one. Jasmine's mother, too, appeared similarly captured as she sat perched on the lip of the sofa, oblivious to everything but what was unfolding on the TV. With a flush of embarrassment, she hoped that her aged mum was not experiencing the same sensations as herself – that would be inappropriate and improper, edging dangerously towards the perverted. Allah forgive. No wonder men did not entirely trust women. Still, they were not their objects to control.

The man soon covered the separating distance and drew abreast of the stationary woman, poised dramatically. With imperious certainty, he reached for her. Animated in the blink of an eye into spontaneous and explosive motion, she spun away, evading his grasp. But then, she executed the unexpected. Instead of running away, she turned on him like an angered cat, hissing, hackles raised, leaping at him in mortal combat, aiming to subdue him to her will. He, in turn, slipped her attack and came back at her with ferocity. The music rose to a crescendo, accompanied by loud clapping hands and shouts of:

'Olay!'

The passion and perfection of the dancers' movements went beyond riveting. They were intimately close, yet never touched, reaching and deflecting, twining one around the other, twisting, sinuous, faster and faster, in time with the music, never missing a step or a beat, never faltering, seeking advantage and dominance. Passion rose from their heated bodies like steam, enveloping the minds and senses of all who watched, stampeding their hormones out of control, releasing their pent up animal instincts. Civilized behaviour is as thin as the clothes we wear on a hot summer's day.

The camera followed them like a predator, always one step behind the chase. It zoomed in on their faces in what seemed like a desperate act to cage these wild spirits, holding them serene and sublimely concentrated.

Cold dampness suddenly seized Jasmine's mind, frigid, suspending her in the space of helpless limbo, transporting away her grasp of reality and time.

Her mother turned, about to make some enthusiastic comment, when she saw the pale, ghostlike face of her daughter, the look she had seen so many times in her homeland when others had received the news of the death of a loved one, a father, a husband, a son. It was the image of cold shock.

'Jasmine! What's the matter? Are you unwell?' she asked, alarm tinging her voice.

'Mum,' came the distant, disembodied reply. 'That's Abdul.'

'What? Where?'

'There, mum. On TV. The dancer.'

Her son, picking the feeling that something was not right from the suddenly changed atmosphere, was looking enquiringly from mother to grandmother, seeking assurances, sensing that he stood forgotten in the charged moment. The two adults sat, unable to give him what he most needed, and this would be one of those childhood memories that would remain seared on his unconscious for the remainder of his life.

'No, it can't be,' replied her mother. 'It's impossible. They are nothing alike. Look. Oh, in Allah's name! There is something there. A resemblance. Oh, mighty Allah. No!'

Her voice drifted off as she stared at the screen, the dancing figures and the crashing music mocking their dislocation. The world dances on no matter the crisis in one's personal life. It does not stop, and it never waits.

CHAPTER XVIII

In this indifferent world, countless people desire more than anything to do good works – to spend a life devoted to a higher aim other than a consumer infested, selfish, dog eat dog society based on a false interpretation of Darwinism. They recognize that others are not as well off or well-placed as they are and would like to correct the imbalance in some humanistic manner. As well-intentioned as these people are, their activities sadly exposes the very privilege on which they stand. They proceed with a lack of knowledge and understanding, sometimes insulting unintentionally the same people they are trying to help. Still, in general, their actions help alleviate the worst of the burdens inflicted upon the uprooted, disenfranchised, dispossessed and homeless that the majority wish to forget or at least ignore.

Shirley was one of these, a member of Jesus' army of earthly angels, willing to dive in, elbows deep, and scrub clean the stains that uncaring humanity inflicts on his fellow man. Her knowledge of the outside world beyond America's boundaries was elementary, and her understanding of its affairs and their ramifications, limited. The corporate-owned news outlets provided her only education through their brainwashing circus entertainment disguised as a global information service and from the mouths of those washed up on her shores. The two sources were not always compatible, and so, being a true red-blooded patriot with a pure heart, she usually conciliated the differences in her birth land's favour. For her, it is far better to try to do something than nothing at all. Unfortunately, she did not consider that when this wheel of fate starts to turn, it could take her to places she did not intend, a passenger, not the driver. Stranded unprepared and displaced, trapped in a circumstance beyond your abilities, is not an ideal position anyone would hope to find themselves. The road of the Good Samaritan remains a hard one to follow and fraught with unforeseen dangers. Who in their right mind would risk everything they hold dear to help someone shunned by all? Only the brave few willing to put feelings before studied social strategy.

Shirley's outlook on life was simplistic and uncomplicated. Her starting point was to see individuals for who they are, free from the baggage of judgement and culture. It was an admirable trait that demanded tough negotiations on personal boundaries – lines that she should not cross or allow anyone else to infringe. God did not make Shirley for angles. She was all circles and rounded corners – open and welcoming. And so, through osmosis, she started a relationship with Abdul.

At first, neither intended to travel down that path. Abdul was a man who never acted on any master plan. He absorbed everything, allowing it to flow through him without resistance, taking the route the winds of fate blew him along. The only thing that mattered for his continuing survival was the Spanish melody. As long as it played in his head, he endured and carried on. Shirley's all-embracing kindness and her green-eyed dancing smile filled with early summer freshness excited the melody and made it play stronger, faster. Abdul followed it, a child to the Pied Piper.

Shirley, on her part, felt drawn and compelled to befriend this placid innocent that was Abdul. She was intrigued by the intelligence and learning buried behind the façade he presented and wanted to discover more. It wasn't a directive but a temptation disguised as a duty. There was something about Abdul that women recognized but men could never see. He had a vulnerability and sensuality wrapped within each other that was nearly impossible to unravel and separate. To try was a lure for many women, something unconscious, a challenge that appealed to them. Abdul also had a talent to please, which overwhelmed and surprised anyone who fell into a relationship with him. He instinctively knew how to satisfy a woman's needs. Abdul was not one layer, he was many, but uniquely, none of them was selfish.

The grey-eyed receptionist with the hard knocks experiences of the world gathered in a knot at her spine watched this ever repeated story unfold. She knew its end before the story truly even began and felt the sorrow of it. She could have taken the protagonists aside and whisper warnings in their ears but instead did nothing. Not because she didn't care but because she already knew that it would not have made one bit of difference. The river was running, and nothing could alter its course before it reached the sea.

Innocent kindness grew into friendship. Mutual attraction developed into creeping clandestine assignations covered by overly casual goodbyes for the public eye. Time spent away together increased until it was evident even to those blinded to such things that the cord that separated the personal and professional lay broken, the ends frayed and tattered. To some, forbidden as it was, there was joy there to celebrate. To others, like the grey-haired receptionist, there was only regret and sorrow to be found, for the outcome was inevitable and written in the stars.

Aware of the atmosphere of disapproval and judgement surrounding her unseemly closeness to Abdul, Shirley stepped up her efforts to make him more American, to strip away that other that made him stand out as unacceptably different. He had to blend in. Otherwise, he would never become respectable.

She enrolled him on English Classes and took him on tours of the monuments and institutions that represented the greatness of America. She began questioning him on the salient points of American history, the Founding Fathers and the Constitution. Shocked by his knowledge which outstripped hers in several areas, she encouraged him to take up courses at the local colleges, which due to his status in the United States, he could claim remuneration.

Eventually, as the fast pace of young people's lives tends to follow, she moved him in with her. She had a small apartment funded through the pockets of overly busy, workaholic parents who lived and worked on the east coast. Like most well off, educated professionals, they thought it best that they should give their grown-up children space and the opportunity to find their way through life without constant interference and micromanagement. The concept was laudable, but Shirley's case led to a degree of overindulgence. The safety net always lying there to catch her allowed the indulgence in an impulsive lifestyle – neither good nor bad precaution. Anyway, bringing Abdul into her intimate space had an unexpected consequence. Naturally, it removed the veil of mystery around her which stood expected in a growing relationship, but with Abdul, it proved destabilizing.

Abdul had mental health issues. No matter his qualities, no one could deny this, and it would be a miracle if he hadn't developed such an illness. He was born in a land with grave uncertainties, a constant and daily challenge. Circumstance had forced him to flee his wife and family to journey, dispossessed and hunted, through a land torn by decades of invasions and warfare. He had endured brutal treatment at the hands of men who had lost their souls in hardening their minds and bodies. With every step, a part of him had diminished. In response, he locked what remained in an iron box and buried it within the deepest recesses of his psyche. The psychologists would not hesitate to label this malady of spirit Post Traumatic Stress. Whatever the science had to say about it, he was damaged, and Shirley did not have the knowledge, the will, nor resources to deal with him in such a state. As the saying goes, 'she had bitten off more than she could chew.'

The trigger to Abdul's last surrender to the physical world that humanity created lay pulled when Shirley revealed what lay beneath her artifice. It was a thing she did automatically, without thinking, as natural as visiting the toilet. It is the wont of a woman to present herself in different guises – a revolving door of clothing, make-up on her face of various shades and design, or not, an alternative colour to her hair depending on her mood or even to lift the emotion. These modifications are meant for her rather than anybody else. The object, to give freshness and rejuvenate what had become routine – an attempt to lift the shadow of staleness.

Abdul's attraction to Shirley was a fragile thing, a fixation on the memory of a green-eyed, dark-haired girl from another realm, one that he was no longer sure was real or not but meant everything to him. Shirley disappeared into the bathroom one day, and an hour later, she emerged blond and blue-eyed. Abdul was devastated. His illusion shattered like breaking glass.

Such a little thing, yet this everyday occurrence was enough to tip the already delicately balanced scales of Abdul's mind off-kilter, a descent into a complete emotional breakdown.

Shirley recognized through his eyes that something of great enormity had happened, a tear she could not repair. Still, women are fixers by nature, and she doubled her efforts to make things right, although she had no idea where this right lay. The answer, in her mind, was just a matter of integration from which would come a sense of belonging. America, after all, was a nation of immigrants. With hard work, everyone could become a citizen.

She found Abdul a job. It was merely a kitchen assistant. However, working your way up from the bottom was the standard progress in this land of opportunity. Rags to riches was not a fairy tale here.

He did what she asked him to do—travelling to and from his night work every day without complaint in the clapped-out car she bought him.

He functioned adequately in all things but in the same mode as an animated corpse would. Then one morning, Shirley woke ill, rushing to the toilet bowl just in time to empty the contents of her stomach. The sign was as evident as the sour stink rising into her nostrils. She was pregnant.

As her stomach grew, so did her mental health deteriorate. She became increasingly unstable and emotional, doing and saying anything destructive to wake up her sleepwalking partner and gain his attention. She even insisted that they be married as she did not want her child to be born a bastard like the father he could never be. Naturally, Abdul did not object, for it was his habit to go along with everything.

From that dark place where their spirits inhabited, every new effort she made only worsened the situation. Not even the beautiful baby girl born into their despairing lives could lighten the descending gloom. Shirley's trapped mind searched daily for a way to escape and finally found a sympathetic ear in which to pour her misery. That ear became her comfort and eventually a lover. She suspected that Abdul knew, but he did not seem to care and continued to carry out his life routine without a break.

Then one morning, he failed to return. Shirley held her breath and watched the ticking clock. After three days, she let out the pent up air and was able to breathe again. Not bothering to report her husband missing, she packed her bags and headed out the door, holding her child's hand, not noticing the tears in her eyes. A girl child will always love her father, no matter the circumstances. It is not he who looks after her but she who instinctively cares for him. Such is the living bond of nature, and not even our unthinking actions can escape its law.

CHAPTER XIX

Abdul held Caterina's hand in his, the blue veins standing out prominently against her pale, white skin – the colour of death. Part of her once vital body, strong and vibrant, was already a corpse, and he could smell the decay from her dying organs. Her eyes, however, dark and beautiful, shone with an inner light, refusing to be dimmed by the encroaching everlasting night as she fixed her remaining strength on him.

Abdul was no stranger to death. He had seen it on the streets of Kabul since a boy and smelt its sweet, sour odour. It had become part of the fabric of life, a curtailment that happened to others. The flies on a corpse were the same as those swarming on a rubbish pile. It was all refuse and food for vermin. Putrefaction on a hot summer's day was merely another colour in the many-faceted prism of life.

The passing of Caterina was different. She had given flesh to his dream, animated it, allowed its expression and made it pure. She wasn't the dream, but she was the essence of it, as close as he could get. His Jasmine was one of the angels, and Caterina was her earthly representative. They were parts of each other – one and the same within the dream. He owed her a debt of gratitude for helping him to keep his mind above the surface of darkness. Without her intervention into his lonely descent, he would have given up by now, his bones turning to dust in a foreign land, unloved and forgotten. Did Allah have room for him? He doubted that. However, for this beauty of the dance, the Almighty would hold her to his bosom. She was a maiden of heaven - even though she was born an infidel. That was no fault of hers. Allah would know that and make amends.

She was holding him fast with her eyes, her spirit searching his for an answer. He felt her need and removed the barrier that protected him, just for a blink of an eye for her to see. She squeezed his hand and smiled, satisfied with her final act in life, a job well done, and slipped through the cracks that were opening at the back of her mind, freeing her soul to fade away. He witnessed her dwindling, the last anchor to this world until she was no more. His eyes remained dry, but inside he wept the tears of a thousand sorrows, his gate that held back the world lay firmly shut once again, but she remained locked there inside him. His last reason for caring had departed, and he had no reason left to care.

He heard the indrawn sob behind him and became conscious of someone else sitting in vigil for the first time. It was the woman who used him for her own ends. The inability to feel did not mean that Abdul was also sightless. He was very much aware of what was happening around him. However, his traumas had left him desensitized in the same way that a drug addict was. A victim, no longer capable of enjoying the sensations fed from his five senses as he once did—one numbed by opiates, the other as protection from unimaginable hurt, both mental and physical.

Abdul knew all he needed to know about this woman. He was not blind, nor was he deaf. He had heard all those damning conversations, and somehow he had filed them away. With the death of Caterina, their relevance and significance became clear and meaningful. Not so much for him, for he did not care, but for Caterina. In using him, this woman abused Caterina. He did not like her, but he did not have the energy to wish her ill will. All she wanted from him was the dance, but the dance lived in his memory which only Caterina could bring into the open. Now she was gone, so was the dance. This woman called Elena would soon find that out for herself. Her ambitions meant nothing to him. She was free to scheme him into her plans as much as she wanted. He desired no part of it. The dance was dead, and so was he.

On observing the Afghan's tenderness towards the dying Caterina, Elena suspected he wasn't as unresponsive to his environment as she had hitherto believed. Was he simply a clever, conniving and patient bastard bidding his time to usurp control of his destiny and the potential fortune awaiting them? Was this broken man merely using her to get to where he wanted, knowing that he couldn't get there on his own? If so, he needed her a damn sight more than she needed him. That was an interesting perspective - the little bastard. Well, she was one step ahead of him. It was time to get up off her fat arse and find a replacement for Caterina. She was sorry that she was gone and would miss her, but the spinning world would not pause for any man or woman. She had to keep moving, or she would miss out on the next opportunity, and there was always one there waiting for some random shit to discover. That person would be her, and no one on this planet could stop her. The key is to keep advancing when the going is good, as every setback is merely a silver lining in that bloody cloud. No one was going to piss on her parade. Not if she could help it.

Elena did all the things that a friend would do for her dear departed. She made preparations for the cremation of Caterina's remains and registered her passing with the relevant authorities and, of course, paid the taxes. Dying like everything else was an expensive undertaking. The actual ceremony was a lonely and sad affair with just her, the Afghan and three of Caterina's ex-students in attendance. Fame, at least, should have given

Caterina more. God knows, she deserved it. She notified Caterina's mother and sister, not that they hadn't already been informed of her terminal condition and were absent at her death's bed despite a phone call from the hospital. Naturally, they were there at the Will's reading and seemed dissatisfied with the division of things. Relatives were always the worst. 'After my very own heart, those two,' mused Elena. 'And I thought I was insensitive. Nothing compared to them, it seems. Well, I am what I am, but those two are something else altogether.'

Having settled Caterina into her grave, Elena turned her attention to the Afghan, who was no help during the funerary proceedings. He had retreated somewhere within his head like a hermit into his cave, preferring not to have any involvement in the real world outside. Well, she would soon put an end to that. He would either earn his keep or risk her kicking him out on his lazy bum. He could find another bar somewhere in this sinful city to while his time away, and it won't be at her expense this time around. Those days were long gone.

With the same attention to detail as an old madam selecting new girls for a king or maybe a top politician, she set about finding a dancer to replace Caterina. After all, the show must go on – it had to go on. She soon discovered that locating a performer with her old friend's skill set was not an easy chore. Caterina was unique – classically trained to the level of a principal dancer, versed in many techniques from the world of traditional dance, proficient in ancient Greek and Spanish folk dance and lore, including Latin dance. She was not merely a dancer but a scholar of dancing, one worthy of a professorship. Her speciality was fusion choreography, and no one was better at it than she was. There was nobody in San Francisco with her pedigree, they told her, and perhaps this extended to the whole of America.

'You'll have to go to Europe, Elena dear, to find what you are looking for.'

Frustrated and furious, she booked her flight to London, leaving an almost comatose Afghan in the care of a specialized private home funded, of course, by his third of their earnings to date. Even this handsome bounty would not last long, considering the cost he was incurring.

'Better off giving him a bottle of scotch and locking him away,' she fretted. 'And much cheaper.'

Elena knew that resurrecting her spectacular performing duo from the ashes was as likely as a Lazarus event straight out of the New Testament. Still, her obsessive, grasping personality insisted that she give it a try.

'Bloody dog with a bone,' she muttered. 'More than likely, they'll bury the dog with me and the bone.'

The Afghan was so far gone up his intestines that not even a surgeon could dig him out. His ever performing again was very low on the tablet of possibilities. All this was evident to her, but she couldn't let it go.

As she boarded her plane, a black cloud of doomed destiny descended over her head and shoulders as enveloping as the smell of the high octane fuel. She had the feeling that she would never see the shores of the United States again. She was wrong in this prophecy.

Abdul dwelled in darkness in a white, brightly glowing, sun-drenched room. He left it only to attend to his basic needs, returning to sit on his chair by the large window with a view of a naturally planted garden dotted with large shaded trees. Abdul would lose himself in the leaves blowing in the wind, the flowing to and fro movements lulling him into his solitude. He felt at peace and found the brightness of the white-uniformed nurse who attended him with a crisp, false professional humour an irritation. Still, nothing of this revealed itself on his serenely composed face. He was waiting on something. He wasn't sure how he would greet it but thought himself ready. Even the melody in his head was more muted, gradually fading into the whispering leaves outside the window.

'You have a visitor, young sir. Isn't that splendid?'

Abdul didn't respond. Who would want to visit him anyway? The dragon, who named herself Caterina's friend, had his door guarded night and day. 'Keep the dogs out,' she had commanded.

Yet it was her teeth marks that lay imprinted on his backside. Still, in the end, nothing of this mattered much to him.

'Abdul?'

There it was, the musical voice from his dream. Usually, it was silent, but now and again, it called to him. He smiled.

'Abdul.'

Jasmine had had a desperate few months filled with polite refusals and downright stonewalling.

'I'm sorry, Madame, but we cannot divulge that information. It is privileged and protected by law.'

She knew that. 'Damn it! But he is my bloody husband, and I saw him on your programme. I need to find him. Surely, you can see why that's important?'

Nothing she said made a difference, and she began to suspect that it was not just a matter of protection but exclusion – the keeping out of outsiders. She had already set her hounds on the case, but they worked so slowly. 'These things take time,' they communicated. 'We are dealing with a cordon of legal issues and must untie the knot carefully.'

'I'm not talking about someone's shoelaces,' she replied caustically by email. 'I'm referring to my husband, missing for years and suddenly appearing like a swan on a dancing show. Find him! That's what I'm paying you for, isn't it?'

They said they first had to verify that he was her husband and not just someone who resembled him – a doppelganger.

'A what?'

They said this performer didn't seem to have a name, and getting access to him was highly complicated. It would take time.

'Time for him to disappear again?'

She wanted to scream, but that wouldn't help the situation. So, she struggled to keep her calm and think things through. Her mother's constant and over-anxious questions didn't help either. She had to refrain from rudely telling her to shut up. Maybe, she should have done that from the beginning because her anxiety-ridden and over-dependent mother blabbed everything to her father like a child when he eventually arrived home.

Naturally, he was sceptical of their discovery, and she could see the words 'silly women' written clearly in his gaze. Then he took the next infuriating route of 'leave this to me.' Why in heaven's name should she? Because he was a man and she a useless woman? She had felt the overwhelming urge there and then to puncture his ego – hitting him fairly and squarely in his financial balls where he considered himself the earner and therefore the breadwinner and the superior man of the household. Were they still in patriarchal Afghanistan? The last time she looked, they had long fled that place of male dominance. 'Well, I believe I am earning far more than you, as a point of interest,' came to her lips, but she swallowed it back as unhelpful bile, as distasteful as that was. In America, money ruled, and she had that tight endpoint already covered in her favour. Gender was the second down in the rankings in thinking if not in legality. Thank, Allah, there were laws against that. There were many things better here than in her home country, and she would use them to her best advantage.

In the end, she had left her father to swim in the pond of his male arrogance. Without a backward glance, she continued to do what she had to do from behind the veil of a woman. Thin as it was, it had a power in it that men had not anticipated and possessed many uses and leverages. The first thing a girl had to learn before she became a woman was how to turn and deflect the desires of men, figuratively and in actuality, and when to do so expediently.

After keeping her biting her nails for a period far too long, her workers in the field came back with the answers she was seeking.

'We've found where they are hiding him,' they reported. 'They, your husband and two women, an accomplished dancer named Caterina Serrano and the team's manager and organiser Elena Lopez, set up a limited company about a year ago. It seems as though the rise to fame was rapid, but so was the fall. Caterina has recently died in her bed from terminal cancer, and Elena has been an unfortunate victim of a crashed commercial flight on its way to London. The plane went down before it could even leave the coast of the United States. There were no survivors. As far as we can tell, Ms Lopez had your husband committed to a private institution for the insane just before her departure. The address is attached to this email.'

Jasmine had not wasted any thoughts or sympathy for the demise of the two women but had immediately departed for the noted destination, leaving little Abdul in the care of his grandmother, to whom she did not bother to explain her sudden actions.

'Abdul? Look at me. It's Jasmine. I'm here for you, my love. I'm sorry it took me so long. I'm here now.'

She hugged his limp body close to hers, her tears wetting his cheeks as she whispered into his ears.

Alarmingly, she felt his body tensing as if he sought to pull away from her embrace and escape. She couldn't understand it. After so many years apart, why was he not happy to see her? Did he blame her for sending him away into the rude clutches of so many brutal horrors? Had she destroyed her Abdul in her impulsive effort to save him? She couldn't bear the thought of finally finding him, only to lose him forever as he fled one more time for safety into the depths of his damaged and tormented mind. How could she have seen him merely a few months ago, dancing like a pagan god of music and now to find a dribbling husk of a man? Was such a transformation possible? She couldn't take him home with her in the state he was in. The triumph of the reunion she had envisioned lay dashed beneath the trampling feet of this new and unanticipated circumstance.

'What has happened to my Abdul?' she asked the nurse. 'Is there a doctor in attendance I can speak with?'

'I'm sorry. The doctors have diagnosed him as suffering from Post-traumatic stress. We've only just learnt his name from your lips. We all referred to him as the Afghan. My apologies, we meant no offence, but it was all we had. The doctor visits twice a week. Your husband is a lovely, gentle man and never gives trouble. I think all he wants is to be left alone to die. I'm sorry.'

Jasmine was about to deliver a harsh rebuke to the nurse. Then she saw the tears also in her eyes and bit back what she was about to say. Life was a bundle of unfairness wrapped up as a gift.

Abdul was afraid. No, he was terrified. The dream was taking control of him. That face that had always lain inside where no one could take it away was now calling him from outside. How was that possible? Was he losing his mind? Was he giving that precious private image to any and everybody? He almost did that with Caterina. But, she was different, and now she was no longer. He had thought himself safe with the comfort of the dream. Was he wrong? He could no longer separate the dream world from the waking world, for they had become the same. His Jasmine could not be in two places at once, for she was either inside him or outside him. He had to choose, but he couldn't hold the images still long enough to do so. He had to find a place in which to hide before it was too late.

EPILOGUE

Kabul has fallen to the Taliban. Even those who expected this did not think it would happen so fast.

The news report blaring out from the TV held them riveted. This broadcast was not about some random country on the other side of the world. It concerned the place they still called home, their birthplace, their culture, friends and family, their past, their land. It was as much a part of them as the country in which they now sheltered and prospered. Perhaps, even more so. It was personal, flooding them with conflicting emotions and a great sense of worry.

Just short of his teenage years, a boy burst into the living room, where they sat entranced. He exuded energy and the restless spirit of youth. The weight his elders carried did not rest on his shoulders. He did not live with a foot in the past and the other in the present. Both of his lay firmly planted in the soils of California like a transported grapevine. It may have had different origins, but the wine made from its fruit was indelibly Californian. He was American, and duality did not exist in his heart. He exactly knew where he belonged.

'Dad, you promised to help me put up the hoop. What's taking you so long?'

The slender man he addressed showed no sign that he was upset or annoyed with the boy's rude interruption. He smiled at him and replied.

'Two minutes, son. That's all I ask. Just two more minutes, and I'll throw a new ball into the bargain.'

Pleased with his successful negotiations, the boy dashed back out to his game.

When the man returned his attention to the TV, his brow creased with inner pain, and a sheen of sweat covered his forehead.

'Are you sure you should be worrying yourself with this, Mr Abdul? It's all behind you. Best to look forward in life, not back.'

She couldn't bring herself to call him by his first name without adding the titular.

'I'm okay, thanks, Nurse Caton. Can't hide forever,' he answered, squeezing the hand of the beautiful green-eyed woman that held his.

'Besides, my bride is here next to me,' he continued.

The woman so mentioned laughed, a pure tingling of sound, like an unidentified melody.

There is panic everywhere, and everyone seems to be rushing to the airport with nothing but the clothes they are wearing. It's chaos, and their fear is palpable in the very air.

'Your mother and aunt will be alright, Abdul. All they have to do is keep their heads down. They're not young girls anymore,' said Jasmine in a reassuring voice.

He nodded absently, knowing what she meant, then said.

'It's not them I'm worried about, to be honest. It's Malik and that old country farmer. They did more for me than any family I had left there.'

She laughed again.

'Malik is a scallywag and a rascal who knows well when to appear like a sheep or a goat. I received another letter from him just this morning - flown out in the hands of some cousin or the other. As for the old farmer you told me about. I wouldn't worry about him either. The old men of our country can look after themselves. They have had a lifetime of sailing through ever-changing and treacherous winds. It's the women left behind that concerns me and not just in Afghanistan. Hypocrisy is alive and well.'

Her mother sitting next to them on the sofa, began to cry. Her father glanced at her and cleared his throat irritably from his position of command in his armchair. For a man of many opinions, all opinionated, he was very subdued and silent. Jasmine gathered from this that whatever pies he had sunk his fingers deep into were now burnt in the oven - served him right.

Abdul, however, was foremost in her thoughts. His health remained fragile, and he had spent the last few years in an excruciating struggle to recovery. When they removed him from his over-expensive care home, they took his nurse with him. Together they all lived in their house on the slopes of Freemont overlooking 'Little Kabul'. Now, there was no going back to their previous existence, not for a long time, anyway. These recent events had put paid to that hope. They were now Americans for good or for foul with no back door left ajar for that just in case moment.

With Jasmine's tender loving care and plenty of hours in therapy, Abdul was slowly emerging from his shell, feeling his way back into the world with delicately probing fingers.

The psychiatrist had cautioned to cushion him from any further shock as best they could, and Jasmine was more than fearful that the social implosion of Kabul would send him scampering back to his hidey-hole. However, he seemed to be taking the dire news much better than most of them in Little Kabul. He held the line with a firmer resolve than people like her mother, who cried after any sudden and unexpected noise.

The best thing from all this was the strong bond developed between Abdul and his young son. It was as if the boy had been silently waiting for his father to return. Now that he had, he was determined not to let him out of his sight for long. Abdul, in turn, had responded to his sons overly possessive demands with patience, calmness and love, qualities that she had not realized he possessed in such abundance. He seemed to be overcompensating for something. What this guarded secret was, she had to wait until Abdul revealed it. So far, there was still a significant part of his story untold. Again, the ever-present psychiatrist warned her not to pry or feel rejected if he avoided specific issues and topics. It would probably take a lifetime of healing, and he would forever carry deep scars. Nothing would ever be as it once was, and she realized that looking forward to a new hitherto unplanned future was the only avenue open to follow. Abdul had spoken briefly of Caterina, a character for whom she could not help but feel a tinge of jealousy, for her importance to her husband was evident in his dark eyes. Still, she sensed the presence of another whose very essence evoked tremendous guilt and remorse in Abdul's soul. She could never get him to speak of this dark gap in his life, and neither, it seemed, could the therapist.

Another phenomenon that manifested itself was the great alarm and terror whenever a melody, primarily Spanish and Eastern music, played aloud. He would virtually run from its sound and, when he couldn't get away, would cover his ears, curl into a ball and rock himself demonically back and forth. This disturbing occurrence made casual visits to Little Kabul almost impossible as this sort of music would blare itself into the public spaces from people's cars and open doorways. It was a huge source of sadness for her as it held a unique and intimate memory, her love of all things Spanish, especially the music and the dance. Now she dared not even mention them. Where this would lead to, she had no idea.

All her energies, when not caring for her two Abduls, she poured into the writing of her book. It was an offering placed before the altar of all the suffering, abuse, and emotional upheaval her people, including herself, had endured over two decades. She told the story in a warm private manner that reached the heart of what it meant to be Afghan despite the twenty or so different tribes that inhabited that tormented country. They all shared a common thread that not even the diverse languages and sometimes to western eyes, ancient and barbaric customs excused under the name of culture could expunge. She may never return to her homeland. And, the heartbreak from this twined itself like a living vine in and around her story. It made her weep. It made her cry, smile and laugh as the words poured out on the pages, for it meant everything to her soul and that of her people.

The End

ABOUT THE AUTHOR

With a long journey of years and distance behind him from when he first started on a small island in the Caribbean to England and finally Italy, the author decided to follow his heart. He turned his hand once again to what he loved most and brought him solace and joy in his youth – books. With his son grown and a new family around him, he graduated from reading into writing – an unimaginable step. His first attempt was 'A Place to Belong To'. He has written eight books since with 'A Memory of the Infidels' Dance', the latest. He is currently working on number nine, a dystopian novel on the last surviving humans in the aftermath of civilisation's fall due to the Climate Emergency.

You can follow the author's work on
https://www.amazon.com/author/jcpereira

https://www.amazon.co.uk/-/e/B07B1KSP6K

https://www.smashwords.com/profile/view/jcpfountain

or visit his Facebook page, 'Something to Read'.
https://www.facebook.com/jcpSomethingToRead/?modal=admin_todo_tour

Printed in Great Britain
by Amazon

68710818R00081